Maybe the Birds

Gold SF

Series editors: Una McCormack and Paul March-Russell

Also in the Gold SF Series

Mathematics for Ladies: Poems on Women in Science
by Jessy Randall
Empathy by Hoa Pham
The Disinformation War by S.J. Groenewegen
The Ghostwriters by M.J. Maloney
The Other Shore by Hoa Pham
Merchant by Alexandra Grunberg
Little Sisters and Other Stories by Vonda N. McIntyre
The Headland by Abi Curtis
Schrödinger's Wife (and other possibilities)
by Pippa Goldschmidt
The Path of Most Resistance: More Poems on Women in Science by Jessy Randall

Maybe the Birds

A. J. Ashworth

Goldsmiths Press

First published in 2025 by Goldsmiths Press
Goldsmiths, University of London, New Cross
London SE14 6NW

Printed and bound by CPI, UK.
Distribution by the MIT Press
Cambridge, Massachusetts, USA and London, England

A CIP record for this book is available from the British Library

ISBN 978-1-915983-38-1 (pbk)
ISBN 978-1-915983-39-8 (ebk)

www.gold.ac.uk/goldsmiths-press

Goldsmiths
UNIVERSITY OF LONDON

Contents

Maybe the Birds

I watch the dog. The dog watches something through the patio doors to the backyard. Every now and then his head tilts to one side in the way it does when I talk to him or sing to him. Although there is no sound that would make him do that now. Not that I can make out anyway. But dogs have better hearing, don't they? They hear things no human ear is capable of detecting.

Like dog whistles.

The low growl of thunder from five miles away.

A million voices screaming from the other side of the world.

Maybe the birds are singing but I just can't hear them. Maybe there is someone out there shuffling about. Maybe, maybe . . . But this is all just wishful thinking – the birds, someone being out there. It's the way your mind gets in the quiet. He's probably just got his eyes on all the brown leaves in the yard and wondering why they're there. 'Why all these brown leaves in the spring, Ma?' I imagine him asking in the human voice I have given to him. But I haven't got any answers. None that he would understand anyway. And so I keep quiet, and just carry on watching as he tilts his head the other way. Not once looking at me. Eyes full on whatever has got his attention through the grey dust coating the glass on the patio door. The little dots of his pupils as black as the night used to be.

*

Every day I tell the dog I will leave him the birds. It's what I do. It's part of our routine now. I get up, get dressed then stand in front of him as he stares up at me from the settee where he and I have been trying to sleep all night and say, 'Well, Sleepy Harry, whatever happens I'm going to leave you the birds, OK? If nothing else you'll get those at least.' And he tilts his head, first one way and then another before jumping down off the settee and sitting at my feet. Not sure what it is I am telling him but hoping, no doubt, it is to do with food. Or perhaps the river – where Richard used to take him sometimes. Or a long walk over the moors on those frosty mornings when his breath would puff out like little ghosts as he ran on ahead of us, searching for rabbits, for rats.

I don't like to go so far with him now though. You never know what might be out there. So I just take him while the sun is still low and murky, then around the fields of dust that used to be yellow with rapeseed at the back of the house. Watching while he sniffs at the shrivelled scrubs of green there, not sure whether he should pee on them or not, if it's alright to do his business on such open ground. But nobody ever comes out of the farmhouse like they used to. And so I just give him the nod, tell him, 'Go on boy, it's OK'. Him looking up at me before lifting a leg or cowering down, the green plants trembling as he wets them, small clouds of grey puffing up from the blighted dry of the land.

*

The dog is not called Harry, despite all the times I refer to him as Sleepy Harry or Barking Harry or, yes, even Dirty Harry. His name is Bear. It's the name Richard gave him because of how he looked when we first went to pick him up from

Cumbria – hair brown and fluffed so it made his face round as a bear's, body fat as a belly filled with fish. He was the only brown pup in the litter, the only one with a longer snout and those brown human eyes. All the other pups were black, same as the mother, more square-faced and short-snouted like the breed is supposed to be. But Bear was different, the odd one out. He was the only one that wasn't spoken for when we got there, but we'd have taken him anyway. And Bear seemed to sense that. He just sat and watched us as the woman talked to us; the other pups pawing and jumping, eager to get our attention. But that little brown misfit was the one for us. He knew it. And those eyes of his told us we were right.

'I think he's a throwback,' the woman said. 'Probably some funny business somewhere, way back, perhaps with an Irish Terrier . . . a Lakeland.'

Richard picked him up, held him. Put his nose down to Bear's mouth until the pink tongue came out and licked at the skin. 'Doesn't matter to us.'

'He's pure though,' she said. 'It's just one of those things. He might look a bit . . .'

'Doesn't matter to us,' Richard said again, scrunching at Bear's ear. The dog stopped licking him before pushing his head back to sniff at something in the air, something neither of us could smell.

The woman scratched the top of her arm, the small bloom of pink there – the first I'd seen on anyone. 'He's a strange one,' she said, scratching harder. 'Those eyes. It's like he can see through you. Makes you feel –', she shivered.

'Maybe you've got something to hide?' I asked with a smile.

She glanced at her arm, pulled at the sleeve of her top. 'No,' she said, serious. 'I haven't. What you see is what you get with me.' Me and Richard glanced at each other, trying not to smirk. She went through to her kitchen then, came back a few minutes later – sleeve all the way back down, a pinprick of blood just visible at the edge of one cuff. 'Aye. What you see is what you get. Don't hide anything, me.'

What you see . . .

Her eyes were not yet glazed as they would have been just a few weeks later, as Richard's own eyes had become not long after the pink first showed itself to him. But we didn't know about any of that then – it was just the very start of things. But we would come to know it before long, when the reports started to come in. First from some small country on the other side of the world that neither of us had heard of. Then from other places too, ones we *had*. Gradually getting nearer. Closer and closer to our own little home.

*

Bear doesn't always follow me into my workshop when we get back from his walk. He often just gets on his bed and curls up with his fluffy dog, pushing his long snout into the near-bald of its belly, his eyes closing to sleep. He knows our routine now. That I will go in there for a few hours and work at the clay on my bench. Making it into small shapes he hasn't seen before. And that when I have a few of them I will leave them to dry for a while before getting the ones from the day before to take to the kiln, placing them on the shelf, ready to fire. Feeding the kiln with wood to get the temperature up. Then keeping it going until day turns to night and the clay starts to set and harden to ceramic.

It might seem gruesome but what I make looks like rows of torsos when you line them up; torsos with thighs, no heads, no arms, no calves, no feet. Just the middles of bodies with all the interesting bits gone. Another way to see them though – a better way, perhaps – is as a wide pipe that separates into two smaller ones lower down, which of course is what they are. But it's hard not to see the body-ness of them. The way they sit humanly in the kiln while the fire licks up around them. The ashes from the wood clinging to the clay – marking each one in a different way, until they are small, pale artworks... only pieces of art that nobody but us is likely to see.

Bear doesn't know it but these shapes are the way I will keep my promise to him – about the birds. He has always loved watching them, listening to them in the time since we got him. So, making my own version of these syrinxes – these bird voice boxes – is how I will keep them alive for him now. That is why I go into my workshop every day and work at them with my fingers, with the fettling knives and loop tools, the wooden moulders and scrapers; to bring the sound of the birds back for us, but ultimately for him. To make the air around the house vibrate with some kind of song once more, after too many weeks of all this silence.

*

I go to my workshop and check over all the fired and finished syrinxes, tilt some of them to see if there are any cracks or chips in the ceramic. Stroke my finger over what should be bony cartilage, those vibrating rings and half-rings that hula hoop their song into life. When I first thought about doing this a couple of weeks ago, after the skies grew quieter, but before the electricity stopped coming through, I searched for photos and articles online about how to make them. Marvelling as I wandered from one page to another at how remarkable the syrinx was – a lower larynx in the chest, different to ours, and which could only be found in birds; an organ which enabled some to sing with two voices at the same time. With air from one lung making one song, air from the other a second. The internet told me the syrinx was an evolutionary wonder, that more research was needed to find out how it had come to be, that there was no evidence of it anywhere else; in non-avian dinosaurs, or crocodiles – the bird's closest living relative. But that research won't happen now. The origins of that larynx will never now be found. It is not the only setback of course. There are so many other things we'll never know. The age of discovery at an end. After all this time. After so many millennia of breakthroughs and progress. So many brains searching for answers.

These syrinxes are not the pots and vases and kitchenware I am used to making – they're new, more of a challenge. Something my hands didn't immediately know how to begin when I first picked up the clay, because there was no muscle memory for them, no felt familiarity. But I wanted to do it if I could – for me, for Bear. And making them was a way to fill these long, slow hours. To make day turn to night, turn to day again. To keep on. Stop my brain from dwelling on what has happened, what might still be happening. To give my fingers something other to do than scratch.

*

I stand back and look over the syrinxes – there are about a hundred of them now. I pick one up and blow into it. It does not, of course, sound completely like birdsong because of the lack of membrane and muscle, the absence of a brain orchestrating things. It is less clear, less acrobatic. More whispery like the memory of that which no longer exists and cannot now be recalled. But it is something. It gives the impression of song at least, of what was. Like those paintings by Monet with their hints of waterlilies and ponds, the poppies at Argenteuil; those ladies whose faces are shadowed by cloud or umbrella. These syrinxes can never be the same as what existed before. They are just my impression of them. My attempt to try and keep some of what was here alive. For us. For whomever or whatever might come across them in whatever future world there might be.

I scratch at my arm now, at the welts and wheals that have risen like swirls of pink dough over the last few days. There are more of them now, on my arms, the tops of my legs, so that almost all the pale skin that was there is gone. Replaced by flame. I go and check my eyes in the bathroom mirror, as I do every few hours, pull the skin down under them. Put my nose to the silver to get as close as I can, searching for any evidence of the glassiness that will no doubt come. But there is nothing except the wide white of my eyes, the brown irises, the full stops of pupils. I let my held breath go and grip the edge of the sink, stare down into the plughole. 'Not yet,' I say. 'Please not yet.' There is a blackness there beyond which light doesn't reach. But I try not to imagine myself falling down into it. Focusing instead on the silver ring around it, the glint of light from the window. I think of Bear and what I need to do for him. I reach for a towel and lift it to cover the mirror. I will do what I have to. Keep making. Keep on. And something else: I will never look into my eyes again.

*

'Come on, boy,' I say. 'Shall we go out?'

He lifts up from the toy dog, head to one side. He doesn't stand at first but before I have chance to speak again he is up and out of his bed, then in the yard. Head turned towards me as he waits for me to follow.

'Hold on,' I say. And go to my workshop. Pick up two of the syrinxes, one in each hand so as to avoid breaking them. So thin they are almost eggshell. I get some string too and scissors, place them in the bib of my dungarees. Then go out to Bear. Stand there and watch him: the waves in his too long hair now, the stub of his tail fat and bushy. His head is still turned back; his eyes never leave mine. 'Come on,' they say to me. 'Don't hang around. There is running to be done, sniffing, finding.' And he is right. There are things we need to do, that *I* need to do. There are things that have yet to be achieved.

I lift one of the syrinxes up and blow into one side, harder then softer. Blow into the other side. A breathy tune that is the ghost of part of a blackbird's song floats up into the air. My chest flutters with recognition. Bear's head tips, and I blow again. He tilts it the other way and wags his tail a little. 'I know this song,' his face tells me. 'Play it to me again.'

His eyes, the way his head moves, brings water to my eyes, a hardness to my throat. It is the same way he often looked when Richard would pick up one of his harmonicas in the quiet of our evenings, softly blowing into it – something slow and mournful: 'Sad hours' or 'Weeping willow blues' or my favourite, 'Moon river'. His long fingers would curve around the front of the instrument, index finger tapping the beat out on top. He would have his eyes closed and there would be deep lines between his eyebrows as he concentrated; his long lashes grazing the tops of his cheeks. Bear would watch and listen for a time, before moving closer to the woodburner then lying down with his legs splayed out at the back; head on his paws as the wood hissed and crackled behind the blackened glass. Richard's gentle playing would make his eyelids lower and then finally close. His paws jumping after a time as he ran in dreams; an occasional half-bark loud enough to wake him. To think we took evenings like that for granted, believing we would always have them. If only we had known. If only there'd been some kind of warning. But then what would we have done? How could we have made those times any more precious than they already were?

'Let's go,' I say to Bear now. He walks up to the gate, looks up as he waits for me to open it. Jumping for my hand in the way he does sometimes when he's excited, eager to run or chase.

In a few days' time I will no longer lock the gate but will instead leave it open. Same as with the patio door. Doing these things to make sure he can run free. There will be other preparations too, like opening all the tins and packets of food and placing them where Bear can get to them; turning the tap on in the back yard so that he will have water for as long as it continues to flow. There will be other things too: squeaky toys hidden for him to find; mine and Richard's clothes taken out of wardrobes and drawers and left around the house, the yard. All of this in the hope he will be OK and that the pink will stay away from his own skin. That he will be one of the lucky ones – if you can call it lucky to survive. This is what I hope at least. What I think of in the long nights. Otherwise what was the point of anything?

We go off into the field, to the edges where the trees are: the black, leafless branches like burned bronchioles against the dusty sky. Bear wanders off, sniffs at the ground, at the withered grasses, as I place everything down next to one of them – one with branches low enough to reach, that I do not need a stepladder for.

I cut a long piece of string and thread it through a hole in one of the syrinxes, tie it around the branch. Hoping as I do that any wind that comes will make the syrinxes sing without smashing them against the bark. I swing it around and it goes full circle, not once touching the tree. 'Thank you,' I say, eyes skyward, speaking to what I don't know. 'Same again for all the rest, please.'

I lift the strung syrinx up to my lips, blow once more. Bear stops sniffing and looks over at me, before carrying on. I do the same with the other syrinx, tying it to a different branch. Blowing it in the same way until a fragment of nightingale wings through the air. Bear runs to me then runs away again, mouth open and panting at this unexpected arrival of sounds he has not heard in weeks. I imagine him thanking me for giving him back the birds – or a version of them at least. His small dog-heart bursting with happiness that there will be more than just weather and the sound of his own breathing in the days and weeks to come.

I pick up the scissors and string, place them in my bib and walk Bear around the edge of the field before coming back home again. Bear stands next to his bed but does not get on it. His eyes follow me. He knows I am not finished yet.

I go into my workshop and find a large tray, place more of the syrinxes on it, take them back out to the trees nearest to home. Blowing into each one before stringing them up on the low branches. One of them the honk of a Canada goose, the other the hu-hoo-hoo of a woodpigeon. Another the skrike of a black-headed gull.

I go back and get more – Bear at my heels all the while. Me hanging them from the branches of other trees as he runs away, runs back again. 'Silly Harry,' I say, before checking the sound of them, the possibility of them hitting the bark should strong winds come. Every time they make a sound; every time they swing without striking wood. There are some blessings left at least. Some things that can still lift the heart.

I hang the last one – the conduit for the song of a robin – and then we go back to the house. Finished for today. Standing at the gate before going inside, the two of us looking out at the grey fields, the jet coloured trees, some of which are now strung with the syrinxes: dark Christmas trees dotted with strange baubles.

Richard's voice is in my head suddenly. The soft sound of it whilst reading to me – as he often would in bed; this time part of Ray Bradbury's story 'The Pedestrian'. About a strange futuristic world where a man is arrested just for going for a walk; where the streets are empty of people, the world void of humanity and warmth. The line that had come to me was my favourite in the whole story. It was the one I waited for, anticipated, if Richard ever decided to read it. The image of a Christmas tree, tall and green and lit up in strings of colour and baubles. My throat tightens as his voice fades and is replaced by the sound of Bear's paws pounding over the land.

'Come on then,' I say to Bear now. And lock the gate, shutting the door as we get inside. Bear going to his bed. Me going to hunt for what I can cook on the camping stove Richard got for us, along with numerous bottles of gas, hundreds of cans and packets of food. Peas, soup, pasta. Tinned peaches that we never would have bought before but which we soon saw as a luxury when everything changed.

Tomorrow I will take more syrinxes out, hang them from the branches of some of the other trees. Taking my stepladder when there are no more I can reach without climbing. Clambering up to loop them around the branches. Making the trees into something more than just the dead things they are; with branches that might no longer run with life but which will bloom with birdsong when the wind blows the right way.

I open a tin of Spaghetti Bolognese, pour it into the pan. Light the camping stove and then place the pan on top. Bear at the doorway to the kitchen as he picks up on the smell of pasta, the sweet tang of tomato sizzling; those small lumps of soya protein and beef hissing from the heat.

After we've eaten, as the night comes, we will get on the settee and I will pick up one of Richard's harmonicas. Touching my lips to the same place his touched, then blowing soft as I can for a few minutes until Bear lowers his head to the blanket; him knowing these sounds are not the songs from before, not even songs at all, but trying to please me by behaving as if they are. Then I will lower the harmonica to the floor and we will lie there in the grey night, my eyes open as I listen for the wind. Waiting for what sounds may come, for sleep. Maybe the birds will sing to us in their new and ghostly way, a strange but welcome kind of lullaby. Bear will raise his head as he hears them. Eyes focused on the patio doors. Wondering why there are sounds like that in the night. When nothing should be singing at all.

Leather

This is how the story begins: with a woman – we don't know her name or what she looks like but we assume she is the heroine of the story – browsing the shelves of a secondhand bookshop in York. The sky is grey through the bookshop window:

pewter, ragged with cloud.

The woman is in the city for a short break but the reason for the break and also why she is there alone are never explained. Words such as *rip* or *torn* are used. More significantly (perhaps), when she leaves the bookshop later, she catches sight of herself in the glass of the door, almost expecting to see:

a reflection of David there behind her, his watery outline.

But we are never told who this David is and he is not mentioned again in the rest of the story. We assume then that she and David have split up or that, possibly (*his watery outline,* for example), he has died. Either way, it is left to us to decide.

It is November. There is the threat of rain. The woman has entered the bookshop on this, her first day in the city, after remembering she has forgotten to bring a book to read in the evenings. The bookshop is described:

the dictionaries, the Dickens; mustiness in her nose, grains of dust on her fingertips.

There is also:

the thrill of leather, the promise of old ink on thin paper.

There is a slight shift in time as the woman thinks over the parts of the city she has already seen as she wandered around before entering the shop: the Minster, the medieval city walls, the Shambles:

that old street once a flesh market home to butchers, and where meat hooks and shelves still hang outside its shops and tearooms.

We wonder about the reference to butchery and if this will mean something as the story progresses – especially as the title of the story is 'Leather'. There is a growing sense of unease although we are not entirely sure where this is coming from. It could be from the language, although it is difficult to pinpoint exactly how the writer is doing this.

We read on, wondering when the inciting incident is going to take place. And it happens then just as the woman picks up a copy of *The Picture of Dorian Gray*, which is sticking out from one of the shelves. She flicks through the novel and finds a rectangle of leather tucked within the pages. It is described as being the same size as the woman's thumb and has two stamped initials on the bottom of it: M. B. We do not know what the initials mean and neither does the woman. We are left with the image of these as well as an image of the woman as she rubs the leather – a bookmark, she presumes – between her thumb and fingers. We are told that she wonders about slipping the book into her bag without paying for it but that she doesn't; instead she goes to the till and then leaves. The light outside the shop is a strange light as she walks out into it. It is the kind of curdled light that comes before a rainstorm, the writer tells us.

*

The action moves to a coffee shop. The woman is holding the bookmark as she reads, absent-mindedly rubbing the leather between her fingers again. There are sections of text interspersed with the story – text from *The Picture of Dorian Gray*:

> **If thought could exercise its influence upon a living organism, might not thought exercise an influence upon dead and inorganic things?**

We may be starting to feel more unsettled because of the references to dead things, leather, butchery. And also because of the fact that the book the heroine is reading is *Dorian Gray*: that story of the young man who sells his soul to stay young, whose sins are recorded on a portrait in a locked room. All of this contributes to the atmosphere but, even though we are a way into it now, we are not sure where the story is leading us.

We are told then that a man at the table next to the woman stands and his wallet drops out of his back pocket. As the man walks away, the woman feels:

> *a dark bloom of push and spark.*

A feeling, we are told, that she has never experienced before. But instead of shouting for the man and telling him what has happened, the woman watches him leave and then leans forward, picks up the wallet and puts it into her bag. She glances around to check she hasn't been seen and she hasn't. We are told then that she has never done anything like this before and so we wonder why she would do this now. We see then that she is still holding onto the leather bookmark, her thumb rubbing over its creases. We start to wonder what exactly this piece of leather is and if, perhaps, it might be more than just a bookmark. But we do not know. All is conjecture.

*

There is a section break then and we next see the woman eating her evening meal at the hotel she is staying at. The book is open beside her plate, the pages weighed down by antique salt and pepper cellars, silver and blue glass. She is eating lamb chops, carrots and potatoes. We are told the lamb is a little bloody. There is another quotation from the novel the woman is reading:

> **... Dorian Gray sat beside me. Some subtle influence passed from him to me...**

The woman finishes her meal and picks the book up. There are couples at some of the other tables but she doesn't want them to feel sorry for her, eating there alone. That is why she has brought the novel along with her. We think of David again and what that earlier reference to him might have meant but we do not know; we can only guess at who he was and what might have happened to him at some point before the story started. When the woman comes to the end of a section, she looks for the bookmark that she has placed in the back of the book, and her breath catches in her throat. The bookmark has grown; it is no longer the size of her thumb:

It skirts the bottom of the page, the initials on it red and sore as brands.

The woman thinks of the wallet and how she was holding the bookmark when she stole it. She starts to wonder if her bad deed has somehow given life to the leather and encouraged it to grow. She dismisses the thought though. Perhaps she has just imagined it has grown. Perhaps she has just imagined the change that she can see in the initials now. Still, she closes the book more forcefully than she intended to and the people on the other tables turn and stare at her. She smiles at them, picks up her book and goes to her room. As she walks up the stairs, we are left with the images of the leather bookmark, the stolen wallet. It is possible we might be starting to see at this point why the writer has chosen *Dorian Gray* as the text within the text. Even so, we are beginning to understand that the story is metafictional rather than realist: the writer is trying to make us aware that what we are reading is a fictional construct. This is especially in evidence when the woman catches sight of herself in a mirror on the stairs and the description of how she looks matches that of the author of the story (we may have seen photos of her on the internet). And, then, when the character chastises herself, she uses the author's name as her own name:

Andrea, stop being silly. It's only a bookmark. You're letting your imagination run away with you.

We are impressed by the writer's cleverness – or, at least, we think we should be impressed – but part of us may also be annoyed at having been pulled out of what might have been an interesting fictional dream, if only we had been allowed to stay in it.

*

We are shown it is night then and that the woman is struggling to sleep. We see her turning from side to side, then getting up and going to the window. There is a lone star in the sky like a speck of glitter on black cloth. She wonders if it might be Jupiter or Venus or Saturn but she doesn't know. We are told the sky was not *her* particular area of interest. Maybe this italicised *her* implies it was the interest of someone else – David perhaps. But we don't know: we are left to our own imaginations once more about this.

The woman goes back to the bed and switches on the lamp. The book is there on the bedside cabinet. She picks it up and finds where the bookmark is. It is no bigger than it was. It has not grown from the last time she saw it. She wonders if she really did imagine the change earlier. She wonders if this dark city in the north of England is having an effect on her mind. Perhaps she should have gone somewhere else on holiday, somewhere warmer, brighter, instead of:

A place that is already starting to bruise and turn towards winter.

The woman starts to read and after a while notices that feeling of *push* and *spark* is there once more. She sees that she is rubbing the leather again between her thumb and forefinger. She hadn't even been aware she was holding it. She puts the book down and gets up. There is a feeling of electricity inside her. She has to do something. She can't just sit there and carry on reading. She has to move, we are told. She has to follow the *push*, the urge.

The woman walks out of her room and goes downstairs. She goes into the dining room where she remembers having used those attractive salt and pepper cellars with their:

twists of silver and blue glass.

She finds a huddle of them on a cabinet at the side of the room and takes a set. She carries them back upstairs with her and hides them in her case. She is breathless, darkly thrilled by what she has done. She sits on the bed then. She stares at the bookmark. She wants to see if anything happens to it, if it grows and spreads. By the next sentence we realise it is no longer night-time though. The morning light is described, the sounds of birds in a nearby tree. The woman has failed to stay awake and she is angry at herself for having done so. She looks at the book next to her on the bed. It has fallen closed sometime during the night, perhaps as she tossed in dreams. But even without opening the pages she can see that something is not right; some change has taken place as she slept. The woman sits tall and picks up the book, blinking against the light:

seeing then how the leather is spilling out from beyond the confines of the book, the skin brighter, more alive – the initials burned into it, vivid as fresh scars.

She had *not* imagined the earlier change to the leather, we are told. It *had* grown in response to her misdeed that first time (the wallet) just as it has done once more (the salt and pepper cellars). She feels sickened, churned to the core. She doesn't know what she should do. The section ends with the woman sitting on the bed with the book in her hands, the leather protruding from it like a pouting lip. Outside, birds skrike and circle in the grey sky through her window. They swoop and rise in such a way that it makes the woman feel light-headed, as if she is spinning a little, losing her balance.

*

In the final section of the story, the woman is back in the dining room, her breakfast untouched before her. The fried eggs:

broken and bleeding yellow onto the plate.

She is thinking of the bookmark, how it is up in her room, still inside the book but no longer contained by its pages. She is wondering what to do, whether she should get rid of it somehow or just keep it, hide it away somewhere – perhaps in a locked room. There is a part of her, perhaps a large part, that is wondering what might happen if she continues. Also, we are told, she quite likes that feeling of *push* and *spark* that comes with rubbing the bookmark. It is delicious to her. She wouldn't like to think that she might never feel that again.

The woman becomes aware of a conversation at the next table then. The husband is reading from a book about York – its stories and mysteries. He is talking about a woman called Mary Bateman.

'The Yorkshire witch,' the man says. 'Criminal and poisoner. Hanged near York Castle in 1809.'

She listens to the man explain how Bateman thieved and swindled over the years, how she was eventually caught after giving poisoned pudding and honey to a couple in order to rid them of a curse (when in reality what she wanted to do was rid them of their possessions and money). The wife died but the husband did not and it was then that Mary Bateman was found out by the authorities and executed.

'After she was dead her body was put on display and two thousand people paid to see it,' the man says. 'Her skin was removed and tanned like leather. It is thought pieces of it were used to bind books and make trinkets.'

By this point we know what the leather bookmark is, what the initials on it mean. But the woman doesn't, not just yet, not until she sees a spot of blood in the egg yolk, not until the man's words start to swirl inside her head like ink in water. In the dining room, the logs on the open fire are crackling and spitting. The woman feels too hot suddenly, too damp on her brow and the back of her neck. She stands and runs upstairs to her room. She picks up *Dorian Gray*, opens the page where the oversized bookmark is. A line of text catches her attention:

Every moment that passes takes something from me, and gives something to it.

The leather feels warm, as if there is hot blood running beneath it, veins pulsing with life. The woman hurries back downstairs. She passes the man and his wife on the landing as they return to their room after breakfast, the York mysteries book still in his hand. She goes into the dining room. It is empty now. There is nobody there but her. We are told the fire is crackling even louder now, the flames licking at the logs as if they are tongues. The woman throws the leather onto the fire, watches it catch at its edges and then she leaves. She cannot stand there and watch it burn. She has done what she wanted to do and now she will go.

The woman goes upstairs, makes her bed and packs her case. She is going home. She doesn't want to stay there any longer. She doesn't know what she might do if she does. The last image we have of her is when she walks past the dining room on her way out but does not look in. She knows the leather is burning. She can smell it. She does not need to look in again to check that it is.

The story is at an end. We are almost at the final sentences now. What the woman does not see, we are told – and therefore what *we* do not see until now – is that the log the leather was resting on has tumbled in the grate, tumbled so much that the leather has been pushed from the flames and is now sitting and cooling beneath the fire, on a slab of stone. The fire has made the leather shrivel though; the initials have shrunken back to the size they were. The final piece of dialogue in the story comes from the cleaner who has come into the dining room to begin to tidy up after breakfast.

'What's this?' she asks, and bends down to pick up what looks like a leather bookmark.

And she puts it in her pocket to take home to her daughter – her daughter who loves to read as much as she does and will appreciate a little gift such as this. It is a beautiful colour of leather, she thinks: the colour of honey, like skin tanned under a Mediterranean sun. The story finishes with the woman patting her pocket where the leather is and starting to tidy away the breakfast plates and cutlery, noticing as she does that there seems to be a set of salt and pepper cellars missing now that she has placed them all back on the cabinet. She counts them again in case she was wrong but she isn't. She will mention it to the owners as she mentions all irregularities, we are told. She will tell them so that they can replace them, if they can be replaced at all.

Later, in one of the rooms, the cleaner finds a book on a bedside cabinet – a book that she recognizes from the title but has never read: 'The Picture of Dorian Gray'. She picks it up and sits on the end of the bed and starts to read it. She is enjoying it, too much perhaps, and now she must get on with her work. She should give the book to the owners, as she does with all items left behind, but she is not sure she wants to: she would like to carry on reading it. She notices then how her other hand has found the bookmark in her pocket and is rubbing it between her fingers. Yes, the bookmark – she had almost forgotten about it but she can use it now to mark her place in the novel before taking it home later to continue reading. The owners don't need to know about any of this: the book and the bookmark. No harm could come from taking them, she was sure of that. No harm could come from it at all.

And that is how this story ends. With the cleaner hiding the book on one of the shelves of her trolley and beginning to spruce up the woman's room, *the cries of the birds through the window outside as hard and sharp as the edges of cleavers.*

Piano

This is not the place she thought she'd return to.

She imagined she'd be with Arthur. Strolling up the promenade as grey, northern skies broke open above them. Or lying beneath him, as he moved over her that first time – the second night of their honeymoon in a B&B in Blackpool.

Perhaps she might have returned to the births of their three children. To the first glimpse of each old face in her arms. Each a miniature Arthur, right down to the wrinkled brows and thin lips, the pale, translucent skin. All of them with long pianists' fingers too, just like her own mother, even though none of them ever played or ever showed any interest in wanting to.

If they had, perhaps things would have been different for her. Better.

But no. Her failing mind has brought her here. To the stage of the concert hall. Standing in the wings and hidden by the curtains – those heavy ripples of yellow velvet which she would touch, if she knew she wouldn't get her hand smacked for it.

Her mother stands just behind her, not touching but close. She can't see her, facing towards the piano as she is, but can feel her, as if the woman is a tall, thin planet at her shoulder. Pulling on her and dark with gravity. Unaware of how she is able to draw in whoever she wants, whenever she wants them – even those she doesn't.

There is a burst of noise from the auditorium, sudden as rain on a tin roof. The announcer looks at her, his hand out towards the piano. He says her name again and then, 'Young pianist extraordinaire', his eyes growing wider each second she fails to move.

Finally, her mother pushes her arm. 'Go on then,' she says, the applause dying. 'And don't embarrass me.'

And she is out, beneath the hot lights, walking towards the piano. Scraping the seat out and sitting down as a sigh of air escapes from a small hole in the side of the cushion. She notices the overwhelming smell of lacquer and, then, how a tiny yellow thread from a duster has become trapped by a hairline crack in one of the keys.

'In a grand piano,' she recalls her mother saying during one of her lessons, 'it's gravity that brings the hammer to a rest after it's hit a string. It helps you play faster.'

But when she tries to lift her hands from her lap to place them in their starting position, nothing happens. It is as if they too are being pulled down by gravity.

'Nobody should have been left there like a sitting duck,' her father said, later. Her mother in the mirror fussed with a curl at the back of her ear.

She'd never had another lesson after that – not from her mother, not from anyone. In all honesty, she'd probably never had the right kind of hands.

One small thing

She is carving dolls for the dead. From lumps of wood that she cuts and pares and smoothes into shape. They're all identical except for the names scored and gouged into their bodies, from neck to foot. Each letter painted in reds and blues. Kjell, Elias, Henrik, Anna, Ingrid. When she's finished there'll be more than thirty of them.

'How are you getting on?' asks Tomas, behind her, at the door to the shed.

He sees how the autumn breeze makes the short, stray hairs which have fallen from her bun shiver against her neck.

She scrapes the knife down a fresh block and a thin peel of wood lifts and curls from the surface before falling to the floor. If she looked down now she would see how it had joined all the other thin slices there like pale yellow feathers. She would see that she is ankle deep in them. She would see them and want to shake her boots clean. He knows this about her; he knows this much.

'OK,' she says, without looking up.

Tomas steps inside and the door scrapes at the ground then stutters to a close. He leans over the table, looks at each doll, each name – lifts one up and turns it left to right, right to left. He touches its small bump of a nose with his thumb, but it's so small it's hardly there.

'Don't,' she says, no longer working the wood. Instead, she is watching him, watching the doll in his hand.

'I just wanted to look,' he says.

‘Well don’t.’ She lowers her head once more, pushing the blade slowly in. Another piece, this time fat as a lip, escapes and falls.

Tomas places the doll down, puts his hands in his pockets. He turns from its blank, dead eyes and stares instead at the crown of Viktoria’s head, at the soft pink of her scalp, scar-coloured against the near-white of her platinum hair. He wonders about placing a hand to her neck, so his thumb can reach towards the swollen rectangle of dressing at the back of her ear. But he pushes his hands deeper into the twin wells of his pockets instead. His fingers finding the loose clumps of fuzz there, rolling them into small, hard balls before pushing them deeper into the seams.

‘How long’s it going to take?’

She bangs the block of wood down on the table in front of her. ‘I don’t know. Christ.’ Spit shoots from her mouth and lands on the back of her hand. It’s a tiny crystal dome which catches the dull light briefly then is gone. She puts the blade down, more softly. Her head is in her hands, the palms pressed into her eyes. The skin on her face reddens. ‘I just want to be on my own. Please.’

He rolls the toe of his trainer over a crisp of wood, then pushes down until it gives and cracks. ‘Fine,’ he says, knowing not to touch her now but instead to leave, across the dry, scratchy, too-long grass, back to the house. To the front room and the TV. To find, not a news channel but a film or music videos and wait for her to come to him. For her to just slip in beside him on the sofa, put her head against his shoulder, just breathe and sleep, breathe and sleep.

*

But she doesn't come then or even soon after. And it's dusk before he hears the door open and Viktoria's boots on the wooden floor. He can already make out the pinpricks of stars through the window. The cratered crescent of the moon scything into the violet sky.

He thinks then of the lapskaus and fresh bread he made while waiting for her. How he pummelled and punched the dough as he stared out at the shed. How he listened for her step as he sliced the vegetables and meat before placing them in the pan. Leaving it all untouched because he wouldn't eat any of it without her. Everything still there now, where he made it. The bread on the chopping board lying cold and brittle. The stew in the pan buried beneath a thick and wrinkled skin of stock.

Tomas turns off the TV and its programme about entropy – that theorised disintegration of everything. He tries not to think of its effect on the world, on everything in it – order slipping to disorder, heat to cold, life to death. How a glass once broken can never jump back into wholeness again.

He gets up, shaking his hands to try and shake the crumbling feeling the programme's given him, like being made of sand. He goes towards the sound of Viktoria and sees her, there in the hallway ahead of him, turning into the kitchen. Some of the hard petals have come in with her and fallen from her boots. They lie abandoned along the skirting or in the dips between the old, oak floorboards. There's the smell of the dolls too, in the air she's moved through, the air she's disturbed. The smell of wood dust, of oil paint.

'Do you want some food?' he asks.

She is pouring water into a tall, thin glass – the only one of its kind left. The others in the set broke months ago. 'I'm not hungry,' she says, turned towards the window. She gulps down water until the glass is empty, streaks of drops clinging to the sides like trails of rain.

Tomas goes to the pan and begins stirring to break up the skin. 'I can warm it up,' he says. 'And there's bread.'

She puts the glass down on the worktop. 'I'm not hungry.' She reaches up to touch the dressing. Her fingers hover over it, getting ready to press.

He stops stirring. 'Is that hurting?'

She turns to him, her eyes glittering in the weak light of a lone spotlight. 'Can I not do anything anymore without you saying something? Is that it from now on?' She bangs the heel of her palm down on the edge of the worktop.

Tomas lets the spoon fall against the side of the pan – a dull ting of sound. 'I'm sorry,' he says. 'I'm just worried.'

Her fingers tap against the dusty surface.

'And how does that help me – you being worried?'

Tomas rubs at the back of his head, scratching what nails he has into his scalp. But with no itch to soothe he doesn't know when to stop. 'Vik,' he says, but can't think of anything else to say.

A humming tugs at his awareness – the sound of an aeroplane lifting out of Trondheim and passing over the house on its way south. He glances out, to try and see its lights blinking across the sky, but all he can see is a milky reflection of the kitchen wall and clock; a pale and half-formed Viktoria – one side of her face and body missing and nothing existing below her waist.

She fills the glass and drinks it down in one again, wiping at her mouth with the sleeve of her jumper. 'Please Tomas, go back to work. For me. Give yourself something else to think about.'

She walks out of the kitchen and up the stairs, Tomas listening to each thump of her boots as she climbs. Realising as he does that the boots haven't walked into their bedroom but have gone instead into the spare room. To its single bed and dust-coated lamp. To be kicked off, not at the side of their bed but at the side of a bed he himself has never slept in. Viktoria's old bed. The one they brought from her parents' house when she moved in last year. The one that's only used now for guests, for visitors.

*

She had left the cafeteria a minute before it happened. One of the few things she'd told him about that day. He'd learned almost everything else from the news reports.

Kristoffer Broch. Third year politics student. Opened fire in the university canteen. Twenty-eight students, four lecturers and a cafeteria worker. All dead. Including, finally, Kristoffer Broch.

There were thirty-three injured. Viktoria was one of them. A single bullet, having missed the body it was aimed at, blasted through one of the large windows which looked out onto a small garden just outside the cafeteria. She could not remember the details but, as Viktoria walked in front of the window towards the garden to take the old leather bookmark out of her novel and read a few pages, a small triangle of glass whipped through the air and embedded itself in the small mound behind her left ear. A dark tributary of blood opening and running down her neck, onto the shoulder and chest of her shirt – a shirt instantly ruined and later incinerated.

In the photo of Broch on the news programmes he was smiling. Wearing a blue jumper and scarf. Unremarkable, except for his striking red hair. The photo was from his student card. He knew because Viktoria's photo was the same – taken in front of a pale green background, the university logo creeping in like a tree branch at one side.

Tomas had been at his father's store as usual, re-stocking the shelves with tins of paint, wire brushes, packs of sandpaper. His father, catching a familiar word on the radio, had turned it up. Shouted over to him.

'Hey, Tomas. It's Vik's university.'

He had wiped at a blank circle ringed with dust, the tin of paint held within it having been bought that morning. 'What about it?' He wiped the dust on the side of his trousers. Blew on his hand to get rid of the last few grains.

His father hadn't answered – too caught up in the news report to speak. Tomas started listening too, heard the words 'shots fired' and 'cafeteria' and, looking at his watch, knew that it would be the time when Viktoria would be getting her lunch, perhaps at that same cafeteria – the one nearest her last class. The one she usually went to.

Tomas had run out of the store, driven his pickup down to the campus. Coming to a stop near the main entrance where the police were stopping anyone from going in. Kristoffer Broch was already dead by then. The blood on Viktoria's shirt was bright but drying. Her wound had been stitched, dressed by a paramedic at the scene, and the skin was beginning to knit.

Driving her home, he had put his hand on her leg – felt the muscle tighten beneath his fingers. She had kept her eyes on the road as she told him about the piece of glass which had hit her. The facts of it. How it had flown through the air and planted itself behind her ear.

'Like a flag,' she said.

Like she'd been marked out and claimed as belonging to Kristoffer Broch. A possession or a piece of land. But most definitely his. No matter whether he was still around or not to make good on his claim.

He hadn't realised at the time that she hadn't mentioned how it hurt, the pain of it. How glass propelled by the force of a bullet must have hurt almost as much as being shot.

He'd only thought a few days later, when he realised her chatter hadn't returned, that she'd described it as if it had happened to someone else. As if she was outside of herself. At a remove. And it was then that he'd started asking her more questions, to try and make her talk – to try and get her back into the groove of herself.

But, as the days had gone on, it felt as if the groove was becoming harder for her to find, so that whatever he did to try and nudge her in only seemed to nudge him further away from her.

*

This is the thought that wakes Tomas in the night, beneath a white wink of moon through the open curtains. The thought that Viktoria has already drifted too far from him to come back. *Entropy made real*, he thinks. *Life to death, love to loss.* Entropy helped along by the trigger finger of Kristoffer Broch.

Without sleep he is black-eyed and aching, but in the morning he decides to walk to his father's store, beneath a September sky filled with clouds the colour of coffee stains. He puts on his apron, begins removing things from shelves, wiping them clean with a damp cloth before putting everything back again, in the same place. As if they'd never moved at all.

‘You OK?’ asks Tomas’s father, grabbing a handful of nails from a box and dropping them into a clear, plastic container – a cracking like hailstones against glass.

Tomas nods. His father nods back. Nothing more is said so he continues, until all the shelves have been wiped, all the tins and packets and tubs removed and then returned. The aisles brighter once the dust is gone. Swiped away. Tomas aware all the while that the shelves won’t stay clean for long, no matter how hard he scrubs at them or how much he wants them to.

*

She saw blood. Lots of it. On the faces and limbs of people she saw running from the canteen. On the bodies of those carried out. Those already dead. He knows because once, while she was in the shed, he'd found her journal and flicked through it. Skimming over the days since the shootings. Looking for some way to read her, to understand how to re-connect.

She had written in red pen, describing in detail what she'd seen. The injured who she recognised, the dead she didn't. How the colour of the blood seemed different for each person. Darker for superficial wounds, brighter for cut arteries.

‘I never really thought about blood before,’ she'd written – the thin paper ruptured where she'd pressed down too hard. ‘Now I think about it all the time.’

As he heard a noise in the kitchen below, he'd put the journal away again. But when he came to look for it the day after, it was no longer there.

*

When he gets home, there's a box on the kitchen table. Viktoria's dolls are piled up inside, facing the ceiling. One on top of another, four rows side by side. Each name burning with the colours of the flag, the red and blue of home. She comes in behind him, lifts the box.

'You finished them?'

She tilts it towards him to show him the answer.

'What are you going to do with them?'

She glances down at the dolls, leans a hip against the table. 'The garden,' she says. 'People are putting things there. To remember.'

Her arms drop a little from the weight. Tomas reaches out to take the box from her but she steps back.

'It's fine,' she says. 'I've got them.'

He watches her take the dolls out to the pickup, putting them on the passenger seat before getting in and reversing out onto the road. Grey smoke swirls from the exhaust as she picks up speed, the pickup growing smaller until it's up the incline and over the brow of the hill, out of sight.

A sudden spurt of fuel within makes Tomas run outside, wheel his old bicycle from the shed and speed down to the campus too. His breath is fire in his lungs, the muscles in his legs speared with pain. Half an hour later he gets off his bike at the campus car park, the pickup slant-parked in a bay but her no longer in it. As he passes by he can hear it ticking towards coolness, the bonnet lukewarm to the touch. He pushes his bike towards the garden – the one near the cafeteria – and stands at a distance behind the thick trunk of a creased old tree, lifting his arm to rest against its dark, raisin-black bark.

She is there, crouched before a patch of soil at the base of a tree, the box at her side. Seven or eight of the dolls are already in place. But she's not alone. There's someone else next to her – also crouching down. One arm bandaged and tied in a sling around his neck. His free hand mirroring the movement of hers as it lifts a doll from the box and pushes it into the black earth. One after another, slow and deliberate. A silent ritual.

Tomas rubs his thumb and finger together fast as he watches them. How they work without speaking. How they're so focused on their task that they don't even look up when a small group of students walk nearby and stop to see what they're doing. They just continue and don't even notice when the students leave.

After a time, the last dolls go in and the two of them stand. They're hesitant before stepping forward to hug. Tomas watches the student's free hand to see if it goes any lower down Viktoria's back, but it doesn't. It stays clenched at her shoulder blade. Balled and umoving.

A security guard in a dark blue parka rounds the corner near the cafeteria windows and the two of them release each other. The guard notices them, stops, but leans back to look up at the wall above the windows, as if checking something, continuing on his rounds before disappearing inside the main campus building. The student walks away, turns back to raise his hand, and is gone.

Viktoria stops watching after him, looks down at the soil once more. The clump of dolls reminds Tomas of bowling pins, set up as if they're waiting to be knocked down by the fast roll of a hard ball. He lowers himself, keeping his hand against the tree to stay steady, and sees how Viktoria stamps on the box, crushing it down until it's just a small, brown rectangle. How she picks it up and pushes it into the open mouth of a bin before heading for the car park.

Tomas sits back on his heels, blinks up at the falling sun. The day beginning to slip into shadow now – day to night, light to dark. The never-ending cycle that will continue each day until entropy wins out.

He begins to think then about the end of things with Viktoria, how it feels inevitable now. Her sitting him down in the kitchen one morning to say she's leaving. That what happened that day wounded more in her than just the flesh at the back of her ear. That she cannot now be the person she was or the girl that he still wants her to be. The one who existed before the massacre. The one who wasn't hit by a hot shard of glass and who didn't see the bloodied bodies of other students being carried from the cafeteria. The one who didn't carve the dead in wood to try and exorcise their lifeless limbs and dead eyes from her thoughts. *She is gone too*, he thinks. *She is dead.*

*

As the light grows dim, Tomas feels a coldness move through him. He stands and stretches his arms and legs to try and get rid of the pins and needles prickling in his veins. Striplights begin to be turned off in the buildings around him, the rooms becoming greyed out and lifeless. Doors bang as groups of students and lone lecturers leave and pass by. Chatter grows and fades. There's the dying growl of cars and motorbikes followed by a silence that descends and builds like snow. The quiet is all around him. And within him now too.

Tomas moves down the grassy slope towards the garden. The soil has become difficult to make out against the surrounding grass. The dolls are visible though – paler against the pitch-coloured background. An assembly of little people, in perfect rows, all facing the same way. Their wood bodies cold and eyes blind in this, their strange, new afterlife.

He thinks of Viktoria again. How she's always sought him out when feeling low; when hurt by a friend's sour remark or a lecturer's sharp tongue. He feels the warmth of her up against him, her breasts pushed into his chest, her arms encircling him. The ragged sound of her breathing as she tries not to cry.

There's a small glimpse of moon then over one of the buildings. Its light falls on the dolls so that it seems as if they're brightening just for him. He realises, as he watches their slight features sharpened by shadows, what he should do – what will make her turn to him once more.

'Forgive me,' he says, and he lifts his foot and begins to kick at them. At their faces and bodies until they're uprooted. Until they're lying at odd angles either still on the patch of soil or out of it completely. Kicking until none of them are standing anymore. Until they're scattered about like dropped pins, covered in mud.

Can you believe what somebody's done? He imagines her saying. He wants to feel the sinking of her body into his. *Some sicko.* Her voice trailing off.

Later, he will drive back to the garden, wash the soil from the dolls' faces, stand them upright again. He'll repair the damage after repairing the two of them. He'll pray and ask the dead for forgiveness once more, because he is not a Kristoffer Broch.

And Viktoria will never know what he did.

*

After a time, he senses something out of the corner of his eye and stops kicking. It's the feeling of being watched. An eye on him, focusing in.

Something makes him look up, to the wall above the cafeteria windows, to a small shape protruding from the stone; a lens reflecting moonlight. A security camera with its eye fixed on him. The light electronic sound of the zoom as it squints to get a better look. Seeing who he is, what he's done.

'Hey,' comes a shout from just beyond the garden. A man's voice interlaced with the scuffing sound of shoes moving fast over concrete.

Tomas makes a run for the tree and his bike. He almost falls over a wheel, recovers and picks the bike up, rolling it away. 'Hey,' comes the voice again, but not in his direction. Whoever it is hasn't seen where he's fled to. He turns to see torchlight flickering over the garden, the beam coming to a rest on the wrecked memorial.

When the beam moves and flashes up into the trees around him, he tries to keep low. Moving slower still so that there's more time between each tick of the chain. Too much noise or movement now and they'd have him.

He makes it out of the campus, through an opening in a wall which leads out to a side road. There are no people or cars about, just the same stillness from the garden.

He starts to pedal in the direction of home, sweat trickling down from his temples. By the time he gets there, the guards will already have phoned the police to report the incident. The tape of him wrecking the garden will be in their hands. They may not know who he is straight away but it won't be long before the video starts to circulate and he's recognised. It may even be Viktoria who phones them – her voice, sharp as ice, as she tells them his name.

*

As he reaches the top of the hill near home, he looks down towards the house. It's in darkness except for a light in the kitchen, a figure just visible as it moves about. He wheels down, nearer, and watches. Viktoria comes to the window and stares out, unable to see anything except her own reflection. She drinks from the glass and tilts her head back for the last mouthful. Rinsing it under the tap but placing it too near the edge of the worktop for it not to slip.

He watches her bend out of sight then stand again, cupping the fragments close to her. Opening out her hands so that the shards fall and rattle into the sink. She stares at her palms for a long time. He wonders if there's blood there – a reminder of the glass and blood she saw that day – but can't see from where he is.

A low, chill wave washes through him, that he can't go in, run the tap and wash her hands clean as she holds still for him. That she won't even let him do that one small thing for her now.

If he carries on watching, he'll see her wash her own hands, roll the glass in paper and drop the bundle into the bin. He'll see her go to the kitchen door, pause and reach up for the light, the house falling into darkness. He'll see how the night takes hold. Of the house, of him, of the town itself. A spreading blackness that blanks out everything it touches. It will be as if there's no light anywhere, no light at all.

The whole world in shadow.

And no signs of life.

Out of body

I think it happens as my eyes open. As the radio starts up at its programmed time. As he reaches across and rubs my thigh through the quilt.

'Are you awake?' he asks. 'Do you want some tea?'

My mouth widens to a yawn. The garlic from last night's takeaway has soured my tongue and taints my breath.

'Please,' I hear myself say. 'I could just do with one.'

I feel like I'm on auto-pilot, not yet here. My eyes blink – once, twice – and the glueyness in them clears a little.

'OK,' he says and leans in. His hand slows on my leg, pressing firmer. Kneading, kneading then moving up.

Again my mouth opens, to speak once more. Words form and build to sound somewhere inside. *Later, sweet, I'm too tired now.* At the same time I can foresee his reaction: that resigned kiss on my head before he scrambles from the bedclothes, his sleepy stumbling to the kitchen for tea and croissants.

But instead my lips and tongue make their own shapes. 'Hmm,' they say. 'That feels nice.'

And my eyes close without me wanting them to so that all I can see is the veil of dark orange caused by the morning sun pushing through the skin of my lids. I try to force them open – to give him a look that says *enough* – but they stay tight shut.

He nuzzles nearer, his forehead and nose nudging at my ear. 'Really?' he asks. There's the glint of surprise in his voice. 'Are you sure?'

I want to say, *No, I'm not sure.* But my head turns, my face pushes in to his. 'Uh huh,' the mouth says. 'Really.' And then my tongue is on his, around his. The lips opening and closing on his. My fingers reach for the knot of fabric at his waist.

While I will my eyes to open and my jaw to snap closed I tell myself I must be having one of those dreams – the kind where you think you've woken up but haven't. So in my head I start to shout, *Wake up!* And then try to scream myself to life. But nothing shifts. My hand does what I don't want it to and moves inside his pyjamas, reaching down towards where there is heat and that hardness instead.

*

I try to retreat deeper inside myself – to shut the doors on a small dark room inside my brain so I can think. Figure out what's going on and find a way out and back to myself. My body writhes and moans; it begs for my attention. But I keep hold of the doors and say, *Think, think.* And then I force myself to see this inner room and to focus on some portion of its blackness while my tongue licks and tastes at the bud of his earlobe.

I think of possession, by demon or alien bodysnatcher. A walk-in, some breaking down of a vital connection in the brain. Maybe I am now my soul, not yet fully returned from sleep – an astral projection still tied to the body by its silver cord but slightly adrift. A broken wing hooked on by tendon. The sail of a boat flying loose. No knowing hand to rein it in, to tether its ropes.

He is on me now, inside me. My eyelids lift up and the dark inner room dissolves. The eyes watch his chest, the delicate curls of hair and the small bumps of flesh at the base of each one. How the eyes watch them move back and forth.

One hand grabs the back of his head, the other splays out on the small of his back. And then I realise that even though I can feel everything – the burn between the thighs, the rub of skin against skin – it is all dulled, deadened. Happening, but on a different level, as if at a remove. Like those scientists who reach into glass cases with the rubber gloves attached to the insides of them, to work with dangerous organisms or to touch the ancient crevices of artefacts or meteorites. Stopping the threat of contamination.

'That's good,' he says, and buries his face into my neck.

'Yes,' the mouth says. 'Yes.'

The eyes close once more as his movements quicken, in the way they always do – making me think of machines locked into their routines. Their actions pre-programmed, pre-determined. No stopping them once they have started their sequence.

And then I think that the body I am now trapped inside of is the same: destined to do what it has been encoded to do. To do what it's doing now, to say these words, then to finish, have a shower, go about its day as planned, and all the days thereafter. Me and it in sync to this point, and only now diverging in what we want at this moment in time.

But what of this me that is thinking now, the me not fully slotted back into its body? Am I stuck here until the silver cord pulls tight and jolts me back in the world? Or am I in an in-between state where I am not yet tied in to that life? In limbo. The place where I could slide from one perspective to another – to a universe where the same life may unfold but differently? Or to another life entirely.

He cries out and slows. His hands squeeze mine. The eyes open again. The lips kiss his neck, the hollow beside his jaw.

Then the arms go around him and pull him tight, the heart pulsing faster when it feels the hard thump of his own.

Then, as I try to envision a parallel world, to see if my imagination is all it would take to shift across, there is a bursting in my mind and body. I cry out and grip him harder. Return fast, with squeezed eyes and balled fists. Born back into myself. The heat in my blood becoming a bonfire.

He strokes my hair and I blink water away from one eye.

'I didn't expect that,' he says. 'You're not usually a morning person.' There is a smile in his voice, bright sparkles of light in the corners of his eyes.

'No,' I say, my voice cracking with newness. 'I'm not.'

He rolls from me, pulls his pyjamas back on. There are patches of pink on his back, in the places where my hands have been, the light red line of a scratch.

'Tea?' he asks, leaning over and kissing me on the forehead.

And then I grab him. Bring him towards me until all his weight is on me, crushing me and making me weak.

'What is it?' he asks, his whole body stiffening. 'Are you OK?'

'I don't know,' I say. 'I'm not sure.'

He lifts up and studies my face, his eyebrows huddling into a frown.

'Did you not notice anything?'

'When?'

'Then.'

'Like what?' he asks. 'What do you mean?'

'Forget it,' I say, and he gets up. Watches me for a moment before peering out at the street through a gap in the curtains. 'Come on,' he says, showing me sunlight. 'That was a beautiful start to a beautiful day. We can do whatever you want. What do you want to do?'

And then he is padding downstairs, making the kettle sigh and the fan in the oven whirr. Soon he will return with a tray. With tea that will scald my lips, croissants that will sit heavy on my tongue. I will sit up and watch him as I drink and eat. Him looking but not seeing anything other than the me he thinks I am. There will be the sound of cars on the street outside. The muffled hum of conversations. There will be the occasional siren. The day too bright now to see the flash of blue through the window though. But I will feel the sirens throughout me. Pulsing. Pushing. Cutting into me in razors of sound.

Small feathers falling

As she walks, the fog retreats. Unhoods itself from buildings and trees, the tall, thin streetlamps craning over the business park – the lights brightening to an aching yellow. Every day her mother phones, tells her not to walk here in the dark. 'I know you've got the dog but you never know who's hanging about. The psychy block's only down the road.' So she tells her mother she'll stay on the main road but goes anyway. She's never seen any strange men here. Never felt her heart jolt at the sound of footsteps behind her. She likes the peacefulness of being in a place after everyone's left, the dark eyes of the windows, the only sound being birds or the scrabbling of rats, the occasional space age hum as a learner driver passes by in the dark.

She once worked as a cleaner in the offices of a sweet factory – only starting her chores once everyone had left for home. Part of her thinks she should have stayed there instead of going off to university for one degree, then another, then another. There was that warm melting inside her as she sprayed polish then slowly swiped a cloth over the desks. The soft buzzing of the lights. The tiny fluttering in her chest as she tipped all her sweepings from the dustpan into the bin bag. There was something satisfying about the quiet, the smell of old carpet being cleaned – satisfying in a way that editing the work of academics hasn't been.

There is a shifting in what remains of the fog up ahead. A slight swirling and parting before huge white wings push through it. An owl with a wingspan wider than anything she's ever seen swoops low and then up over the blue metal gates of a factory and is gone. The dog stiffens and pulls on the lead, barks once in its direction and is silent again.

'Oh,' she says, without meaning to. Then, 'Ridiculous.' Not sure what she means – that her reaction is ridiculous or the appearance of an owl in the middle of a business park is. She laughs and the dog turns towards her before looking above the gates once more. 'Well, that was a surprise, wasn't it, lad?'

The dog turns again before getting the scent of something in the grit and litter under the bushes and pulling her on, his snout sniffing and snuffling in the dirt.

'Terrier?' a voice behind her asks.

She turns to find a man in a dark suit walking towards her, all angles and sharp edges – a tie pulled tight at the throat. 'Aye,' she says.

'Sorry. I'll just…' and he points to the road, steps off the path and into it, further away from her. 'Men shouldn't walk behind women out on their own, should they? I read something about it, about showing you're not a threat.' The nearby streetlamp shines on the man's hair, which is black and gleaming; so black it has a slight sheen of blue to it; his beard the same. 'Nature's sniffer dogs, eh?'

'Oh yeah. He's only happy when he's sniffing for stuff. Food usually.'

'Or prey?' the man smiles. 'That breed, at least.' His eyes are clear as raindrops; raindrops falling from a dust-grey sky.

'Very true. That's why I rarely let him off. He'd get the scent of something and be away. I'd never see him again.'

'Ha,' he says. 'And that's why we keep them tethered to us, isn't it? Because they'd leave us otherwise.' His irises darken for a moment before starting to brighten once more.

She smiles. 'And on that cheerful note…'

He laughs, shakes his head. 'Sorry,' he says. 'Just going to the dark side… I'm B.'

'As in the letter or…?'

'Yes.' He strokes his beard and a flash of ice streaks across his eyes; a firework reflected. She glances behind, scans up into the night, but there is no trace of it now. 'It's short for Bertrand. My mother was French… she wanted something that reminded her of home, so that's why. But I prefer B, so…'

She nods and her eyes catch on a thick loop of gold chain hanging out over the knot of his tie. As soon as she sees it, he pushes it back out of sight, then swipes his finger around the inside of his collar as if to make sure it's gone. 'OK, Just B. It's more interesting than Roger or Geoff I suppose. Not that people called Roger or Geoff aren't interesting, you know… but… well, the names…' She knows she is waffling but can't seem to stop herself.

'And you are?' He raises his eyebrows, his small mouth partly open – thin lips glistening in the half-light.

The dog moonwalks out from under a hedge and stares up at him before lowering his back end and sitting on the pavement. 'Well, he's Mister and I'm Mel. We come as a pair. Well, you know… we… we're like…he's…' She presses her lips together with thumb and forefinger, the words stalling behind her teeth.

'Mel?' His mouth makes a chewing motion for a moment like he's tasting the word, savouring it. Then he stops and smiles. 'And what's that short for?'

She puts a hand to her hip, raises an eyebrow. 'Oh, that's for me to know…'

'And for me to find out… in whatever way I can.' He scratches along his jawline, eyes skimming over her body – breasts, waist, the light curve of her hips – before coming to a rest on Mister, the side of one nostril flaring. 'Do you always talk to strange men in business parks at night?' He pushes a hand through his hair, the movement sending blue electricity shivering through it.

'Are you a strange man?'

He straightens. 'Some might say I am, but no. At least I don't think so.'

His voice is cool, a little monotone, but not in an unpleasant way. 'Strange or not,' she says. 'I've never seen you on here before.'

'Well, that's because we've never explored this place before. I have a business here, marketing, branding' – he nods towards the centre of the business park – 'but we just fancied having a little wander about, so…'

'We?' she asks, remembering now what B had said. *That's why we keep them tethered to us. They'd leave us otherwise.* But what is tethered to him? She scans his boots, his legs, his hands at his side but there are no ropes or leads or anything that is tying him to something else.

B glances up into the sky then, eyes skimming the branches of the nearest trees, the tops of the closest buildings – 'My girl,' he says, pulling something out of an inside pocket of his jacket. 'She'll be back any time.'

She looks around now too but there's only the two of them and Mister, just the light whisper of a coming breeze.

'Teddy,' he says, then widens his mouth, the shadows on his face making her heart stumble for a moment. At first, there is nothing but the sound of his breathing, the small lumping of a pulse in his neck. She shifts from one foot to another, not sure what he's doing. Then his Adam's apple lifts in his throat and there is a screeching – a breathy 'waaaah' that wings up and over his tongue, growing louder and louder until it ricochets from the nearest building; so loud it makes her put a finger into her ear. Mister stands and barks and B closes his mouth again, eyes scanning the air once more. 'Ah,' he says, sensing something she can't see. 'Here she is. Here's my Teddy now.'

She glances around but all is still. There is just the last patch of mist slipping away down the side of a building, the sudden flickering of the streetlamp nearest to them. Just then though – as B pulls a thick glove onto one hand, opening and closing his fist inside it as he does – there is a coolness on the top of her head, the lightest ruffling of her hair. And there are wings and whiteness then at the edge of her vision, the skim and swoop of feathers and feet. But no sound at all. B lifts his hand and there is an owl here, lowering her talons to it and gripping the leather before folding huge wings into a soft, speckled body.

'Teddy,' he says, as the bird nibbles at the base of one gloved finger. 'My girl.' Teddy lifts the thin brown heart of her face from the glove, looks at Mel then B before opening her beak and hissing at him, hard. Out of the corner of her eyes, Mel thinks she sees B tighten the leather around the bird's talons, squeezing until she stops making the sound, her beak still wide but quiet. When she glances down to check though, he doesn't seem to be squeezing at all.

'Oh,' says Mel, not liking the small, pink cave of the bird's silent mouth, the way she is trying to lift her legs away from the glove.

'She should know not to screech at me,' he says, as Teddy lowers her head. 'Shouldn't you, girl?' The bird lifts her head, her beak closed now – the pink cave no longer visible.

'Oh… is that… is she…?' But she is not sure what she wants to ask apart from if Teddy is OK – but she closes her mouth, feeling it is not her place to say anything. Teddy turns towards her and blinks before turning away again.

'Good girl,' he says, stroking the top of a foot. 'My good girl.' He continues, the bird settling. Teddy's head swivels towards Mister. 'Well, I suppose we'd better head off. Just a brief fly out tonight.'

Mel nods and Mister stands, ready to continue his walk. B keeps his hand up, Teddy opening her wings out to steady herself as he starts to walk away with her. As he reaches an SUV parked in the murk beneath a broken streetlamp on the opposite side of the road, he opens the boot and fiddles with the door of a cage. But before he puts Teddy into it, he turns back to Mel. 'We're going now but you'll meet me for coffee tomorrow.'

A laugh tumbles out of her throat without her meaning it to. And – because of the blue light in his hair, the grey of his raindrop eyes – there is an electric thrum between her legs, like the plucking of a string. 'Oh, will I?' she asks, pushing her shoulders back.

'Yes,' he says, Teddy flapping her wings as he places her inside the cage and closes the door. 'You'll meet me for coffee and then… we'll see.'

'Is that right?'

'So, 3pm at The Coffee Pot.' He stands and stares at her, as he bites his lip and pulls the glove from his hand. 'Say, "Yes, I'll be there, B".'

And, despite feeling she should say no, the words somehow slip out over the warm, wet tip of her tongue. 'I'll be there.'

'Yes,' he says. 'B.'

She stares at him. 'Yes,' she says, 'B.'

And then the man slips the glove back into his pocket, gets in his car and leaves.

*

There was coffee, yes. Then more coffees, meals and, a few weeks later, a weekend stay in a cold castle on the Yorkshire coast; the grey sea husky through the stone walls. In the day, they toured ruins, walked the coastline, had long lunches with bottles of wine. Mister with her mother; Teddy in a cage in the shadowed corner of the dining room. At night, he cooked for Mel with the food they'd bought during the day – fresh fish, limes, blocks of near-black chocolate; eating while seated at either end of a long table. A low fire crackling in the hearth, cutlery clicking in the quietness.

'Are you not eating?' she said to him on the second night, as he watched her spooning chilli lime fish into her mouth, followed by dark chocolate pudding – his fork hovering above an untouched plate.

'I like that you have an appetite,' he said, a tine scraping at the tuna. 'I like my women to eat what I put in front of them.'

She laughed. 'Ooh, *my women*? How many have you got… apart from Teddy?' Her breath caught in her throat at his high cheekbones, the slick pink of his bottom lip. She imagined the bird's head swivelling underneath the blanket covering her cage, goosebumps rising and falling along the exposed flesh of her arm.

He beamed and lowered his head. 'Oh, you know… just a few.' He leaned forward and stared into her eyes. 'Bad ones, the lot of them… unlike you.'

'I can be bad,' she said, her head swimming from the wine, 'if you want me to be.' She raised an eyebrow at him. 'If that's what you like.'

He lowered his fork to the plate, let it fall. A shard of cold light in his eyes. 'I don't,' he said, his features sharpening. 'I like my women to be good.'

Her stomach roiled at his sudden cooling, the food bitter and heavy inside her. She thought they had been joking – about *his* women, their badness – but now she wasn't so sure. She remembered, then, how she thought he had held Teddy's foot that first night, how the bird had screeched. She remembered how his nostril had flared as he looked down at Mister on the pavement. Images she had tried to brush away like spots in her vision. Her heart seized. She missed her dog. Wanted to go home, ruffle the scrags of his coat. Then B smiled and moved towards her, heat radiating from all the places not covered by clothes – wrist, forearm, the side of his neck – until she doubted the coldness had ever even been there.

'You should wear blue more often,' he said then, eyes lowered to the dress she'd bought especially for the weekend; her shoulders bare, little spatters of white in the pattern. 'It's your colour.' It was then that he stepped closer and held his hand out to her. She hesitated for a moment – the dark chocolate still curdling inside her – but when she raised her own, her fingers reddening at the warmth of his skin, the swirling and heaviness lifted from her until she wasn't sure it had been there at all.

*

'You're different,' her mother said, when she called to pick Mister up in her boots and jeans, a blue blouse that B had bought for her while they were away. 'Did something happen?'

'No, not at all,' she said. 'What do you mean?'

Her mother scrunched her eyes up, gaze moving down to Mel's boots then up to her blouse before coming to a rest on her face. 'Don't know. You tell me.'

'Don't be so suspicious!'

'I'm not suspicious,' she said, clicking the lead into Mister's harness and handing it to her. 'I'm just not blind.'

'Right,' Mel said, taking the lead and walking the dog to the front door. 'Well, I had a nice time.'

'Good,' she said. 'I hope you did.'

'Of course I did,' she said, encouraging Mister up into the passenger seat and clicking his safety clip into his harness. 'Why wouldn't I have?'

Her mother shrugged. 'You tell me.'

'Dear oh dear,' she said, shaking her head as her mother rubbed the top of her arm.

Then, a few days later, when her mother came to sit Mister while Mel went on a day trip to the Lakes with B, she eyed her daughter's loose blue dungarees, the paisley scarf around her neck. 'You're wearing a lot of blue all of a sudden,' she said. 'I thought you didn't like it?'

Mel put a finger in the gap between her neck and the silk, pulling it so it wasn't as close to her throat. 'I've literally never said that. I like blue… always have.'

'Right,' her mother said, standing back with a hand on her hip. 'Well, you be careful.'

Mel rolled her eyes. 'Course… he's perfectly safe, you know… he's fine.'

'Uh huh.' Her mother moved to the window, folded her arms as she peered out at the SUV ticking over at her front door. 'One day you might have a daughter,' she said. 'And then you'll know.

'OK.'

'Until then… just you be careful.'

*

Mel and B had walked only a small way around Lake Windermere when the air thickened and the rains came; little stabs of water that pierced her jacket and seeped into her armpits and groin. They dashed back to his car, parked in a space near to the little theatre there – their tickets for the play version of *The Shining* stored on her phone for later. B folded his jacket into the boot and changed his trousers and shoes before climbing into the driver's seat. Mel got in without changing anything, shaking her head and laughing at how soaked they were – droplets of water spraying onto the dashboard and runnelling into the moat at the bottom of the gearstick.

'Don't do that, you idiot,' he said as he watched her, blue-black eyebrows knotting before opening the glove compartment and taking out tissues – wiping until all traces of the water were gone.

She took a sharp breath in; the lightness draining from her and replaced by the feeling of having lost her footing somehow although she wasn't sure how. 'I… Sorry,' she said, lifting up and taking her jacket off, placing it next to her feet. Then glancing around, unsure whether she was still leaving water somewhere without realising it.

'Fucking wally,' he said, with a shake of his head. 'Jesus.'

The names – *idiot, wally* – became dark moths in her head. She tried to shoo them away, pretend they weren't there. Told herself she was being too sensitive, as an ex had said more than once. But they wouldn't leave. Instead it seemed as if they wanted to stay. 'Sorry.' Then quieter. 'It's only water.'

He stared at her. '*It's only water.* Do it in your own car, *love* – not mine.' He swiped a small dot of wet from the dashboard with his sleeve, tutted. Straightened his cuffs and let his hands hang over the top of the steering wheel.

The rain fell harder then, making watercolours of the world outside. Everything a blur of greens and greys, the odd smudge of red. Her heart was thumping so hard she tried to slow her breathing to soften it but couldn't. The insides of the windows turned to fog.

'Anyway, we'd better go,' he said, after sitting in silence for a while – the rain slackening off now. 'I need a drink.' He got out without waiting for her, running for the shelter of the theatre door. Standing there with his arms folded until she got out and went over too. He lifted his key and pressed it, the lights on the car flashing once, and then again. As he turned and went in without saying anything to her, he held his hand out behind for her to take it, but she turned her head towards the theatre bar, pretended she hadn't seen it hovering there for her.

*

There was strangeness and silence, shouting and running but she couldn't latch on to the threads of the play long enough to follow what was going on. There was a husband and wife looking after a remote hotel in winter, a boy that could see spirits. At one point the man was reading *Bluebeard* to the child, the next he was typing the same words over and over, then chasing his wife with an axe. But she couldn't untangle the knots of what any of them were doing and saying to each other; she had missed too many stepping stones in the plot. The moths circled in her brain as she watched, tickling the backs of her eyes, the insides of her skull. She tilted her head one way and then another to try and shift them, but there was nothing she could do to make them go.

At one point, B's eyes were on her. Then he nudged her thigh. She turned to him – noticing how he was all sparkle-eye and warmth then. He nodded down to her lap. His hand there, fingers open, waiting for hers to join his. She hadn't even felt the weight of it. He bent down and kissed her shoulder and a small pebble shifted in her chest even though she didn't want it to; an automatic response to his eyes, the ripeness of his bottom lip, the memory of how he had called her pretty earlier in the day. A vein of heat opened and ran through her and she found herself moving her hand, entwining her fingers with his as the set changed to become a snowy maze; as the play blazed and burned towards its end.

'He's warmer than David ever was,' she remembered saying to her mother, after the trip to the castle – remembering the one thing she had always craved from her ex but never got: affection, romance, someone who would hold open the door for her – literally, metaphorically, as B had been doing. 'And he cooks for me.' But the moths were there even then – had been from that night in the business park. Just one at first, then more of them. Clustering. Cluttering her mind. She just didn't want them to be. She wanted to be wrong about them. She wanted this to be a good thing.

By the time the play ended, the rain had stopped, and they walked back to the car, holding hands – his thumb stroking hers, his pupils dilated so wide they almost covered the grey of his irises. She climbed inside, checked her hair and clothes for raindrops before settling back into the seat. She was tense, tight. Didn't want to do anything that would bring the iciness back. B leaned across and put a fingertip to her jaw, a sudden, surprising wetness between her legs. Then his mouth was on hers – all slick and slip, his tongue moving over her tongue. His hand moving from her face to her breast then her thigh, before moving back up and softly holding her throat.

'Gorgeous girl,' he said, his voice breathy.

'Oh really?' she asked. In all their years together, David had never once called her gorgeous or pretty. Had never cuddled her in bed. Never shown anything much in the way of passion for her. Two years in and he had stopped wanting to make love to her altogether.

B nodded, carried on kissing her – the wetness turning to flame now. The windows whitening from the intensity of their breathing, but she was glad of it now. There were people still milling about in the car park; people who might tut at such a display. She didn't want to be seen; for people to be witnessing what was happening here.

He kissed her harder then, tightened his hand at her throat. 'What do you think about this?' he asked, his voice hoarse. 'Would you like to be strangled, do you think?'

She swallowed and pulled back, blinked at him. The flame dowsed. She wasn't sure she'd heard him right. Too much blood was thundering in her ears.

'Would you?' He sat back, watching her before shaking his head. 'Don't freak out.'

'Don't freak out?'

He held his hands up. 'An ex of mine liked it, that's all.' He fiddled with the key in the ignition then put his hands on the wheel. 'I'd do it… if you wanted me to. *During*… you know.' He nodded down towards her thighs. 'If you wanted,' he said, as if he was offering something as mundane as walking the dog.

She scratched her head, the moths peppering her brain with dust. 'I don't… why would anyone want you to do that to them? I don't understand why *she'd* want that, if she did…?'

'*If* she did?' He raised his eyebrows. 'What's that meant to mean?' He stared at her.

'No, I mean… I just mean if she wanted that, why would she? Why would anyone?'

'*I* don't know,' he said, wiping a hand over his beard then putting the car into gear. 'God. People are weird.' He shrugged. 'Don't be uptight about it. I think it turned her on. It might turn *you* on.'

I could think of better turn-ons, she thought, but didn't say. 'I don't think so. And I'm not uptight, I'm just pretty vanilla… so, no – not for me. No.'

'Vanilla.' He nodded, lifted his foot from the clutch and pulled away, out of the car park and towards the M6. The clouds turning to clumps of candyfloss ahead of them. 'We'll see… I have a sixth sense about things like that.' He side-eyed her, then smirked.

'You don't,' she said, without smiling, and touched the front of her neck where his fingers had been. Tried not to feel the heat from them.

'Whatever you say… but I do.'

'I mean it,' she said. 'You don't.'

On the drive back he kept his hand on her thigh, pummelling it every now and again. She wanted to ask how he could strangle someone for sexual kicks, how – if it wasn't his idea – he could go even along with it. What in him would want him to make someone struggle for air – especially when that person was someone he was supposed to love, or at least have some kind of feeling for? The questions brought other questions. Ones about his occasional coldness towards her, the sudden moments of snappiness that made her stomach twist, but every time she thought of bringing them up he turned and smiled at her; the words turning to ashes on her tongue.

'I need to go away for a few days,' he said, as they got nearer to her house – a seam of light breaking through a rip in the clouds, making her think of kintsugi: those broken pieces of Japanese pottery whose joins were repaired with gold lacquer. Disaster turned into art. 'Will you housesit for me? Keep an eye on things?'

'You're going away?'

'Yeah, business… I need to go and speak with a potential new customer. A biggie in the US. I'll only be a few days.'

'You mean, I'll actually be allowed to see where you live?'

He dropped his head back, laughed. '*Allowed.* Hey, it takes a while for me to trust. I can't just have anyone coming over, you know. But yeah, you're allowed.'

'Ooh, I'm honoured,' she said.

'I'll bring you something nice back?'

'Oh,' she said, remembering how David never bought her anything if he went away on his own, how he sometimes wouldn't even text her.

'I'll stock up for you – all the things you like?' He batted his eyelashes at her until she smiled at him, the air in the car clearer now.

'Oh, go on then. And Teddy?'

He waved a hand. 'Oh… she'll be with a friend of mine. She'll be fine, so yep… just the house.' She nodded and his hand squeezed her thigh. 'I'll miss you,' he said. 'My good girl.'

She stared at him, not sure if he was joking or not, trying to wind her up. Then he turned, a smile flickering at the edges of his lips, and she slapped him playfully on the arm. '*My good girl.*'

'Well, you are,' he said, his pupils smaller now – the grey emerging from behind the black, like the end of an eclipse. 'And you know I like my women to be good.'

'Bugger off,' she said. 'But yes, OK, I'll do it.'

'Bring that mutt if you want to. As long as it doesn't shit all over the place.'

The moths grew lively again, tapping against her skull until a headache started to form there. 'It?'

'Joke,' he said, without a smile. 'No need to get all protective of him. Of course, you can bring him. Just make sure he behaves though, eh? I don't want to come back to God knows what.'

*

She stays the night before he leaves for America – in his house of glass and metal, on the edge of town and with only trees and trails for company. It is white and angled, as she suspected it might be. Not a hint of dust or crumb anywhere. Not a crack in wood or paintwork, unlike her own house. After she arrives, she shrinks as she skirts the edges of worktops and tables, keeps the dog on a short lead, swiping her foot over the places where Mister leaves smudges of mud on a floor tile.

'Here,' B says, giving her a key card. 'This is for the house, to get you in and out. It locks automatically once you're inside.'

'Gosh,' she says, 'hi-tech.'

'Can't be too careful.' He holds finger and thumb to his chin then, begins pulling at the hairs there. 'There are no other locks inside, except one.' He tilts his head and starts walking down a corridor. 'Here,' he says. 'I'll show you.' He stops outside a door with a small, black pad on the wall beside the handle – an illuminated red dot on it. 'The card opens this too… but I don't want you to go in here. It's just things I've collected over the years… private things. I'm only showing you in case you get curious and decide to have a look inside.' He holds a hand to his chest, his eyes with a sad, grey sheen to them now. 'But don't. OK? It's just personal stuff. You can go anywhere else… just not here.'

She pushes questions away, rubs at the creases that are forming between her eyebrows. 'OK… not if you don't want me to.'

'I don't,' he says. 'My good girl.' He side-eyes her and smirks, the grey sheen no longer there now.

She shakes her head.

'Well, I suppose we'd better get to bed,' he says, yawning. 'Early start tomorrow for some of us.'

She nods, puts Mister on his bed in the kitchen, and takes her case to the bedroom. She changes into new, blue pyjamas in B's en-suite; they are the colour of periwinkles and thin and silky as spiderweb.

When she comes out, he's standing there, next to the bed. 'Lovely,' he says. 'I'm glad you… listen to me. It's your colour, this. Definitely your colour, gorgeous girl.'

And then his hands are at her waist and he's kissing and lowering her to the crisp white of the bed, unbuttoning the pyjamas that she's only just slipped on. He kisses her jaw, her neck, as air catches in her throat. She listens for Mister in the kitchen but there is nothing; the only sound now an occasional light metallic clinking that is coming from somewhere else, some distant part of the house.

*

In the morning, she blinks awake to speckles of light in her eyes, on her skin, as the sun filters through leaves of oak and sycamore from the woods beyond B's house. Dusting her with gold that seeps down through epidermis and dermis, then through to tissue, to muscle, to bone.

He is gone. She doesn't know when, didn't hear or feel him go. Just knows from the airy silence that fills the room that B is no longer here – the atmosphere cleaner, lighter somehow, easier to breathe in. He is either at the airport now or already part of the way into his flight to the US, depending on the time. She is alone, except for Mister in the kitchen. Alone. And something about that knowledge makes her spread her arms and legs wide now to find the coldest parts of the bed. Keeping them there until her limbs begin to cool, the heat transferring from skin to sheet as she stares at the blank white of the ceiling.

She turns, checks her phone. Seven am. She is up and dressed and down with Mister by half past. Him off his bed and at her feet, sitting and staring until she gives him his breakfast, then at the glass door staring out towards the trees. She puts her jacket on, takes her charged phone, the keycard – grabs Mister's lead and out they go into sunlight, walking until they are buzzing with it; the light breeze moving through the green like someone breathing on the back of her neck.

They walk for three miles before finding themselves back at the house, Mel not sure whether they've walked in a circle or somehow doubled back on themselves. She finds the keycard in her pocket, then lifts it to the black pad next to the door, the light flicking from red to green. She opens it and they go inside, then when she closes it again, there is a mechanical sliding as the lock slips home. A twisting of rope in her stomach and she puts the card on the internal pad to make sure it will open again – it does – locking again when she fails to open it five seconds later. Shhhh. The sound echoing from the white tiles and glass. Shhhh. Shhhh. Shhhh.

The day opens out like a clear path before her – no work, no other commitments – and so she watches TV, starts a book that's been sitting on her shelf for years (Oscar Wilde), cooks food, walks the dog again and still it is only 3pm. Time moves slower here. She yawns, stretches out on the sofa, snoozes. When she wakes, she is sure she's been asleep for hours but it's only 3.20pm. Mister is off his bed and sitting next to her, looking towards the corridor, head tilting from one side to the other in the way he does when he hears a sound he's not sure of. She sits up and listens: it is the same metallic clinking from the night before. Not rhythmic or repetitive; not following a particular pattern like the drip of a tap. Instead it is a light clanking, then silence, then more clanking – like some small kind of chaos is happening somewhere not too far away from them.

The keycard digs into her hip and she rolls to a stand, pulling it from her pocket, rubbing the place where it has cut a line into her skin. She clutches it in her hand, then listens and moves towards the sound, Mister at her heels, head low, following it down the corridor to the door with the black pad next to the handle. All is quiet now except for the slight hum of something electrical somewhere behind the wood; a light or a machine, plugged in and pulling current in and through it. There is the clinking again and she leans into the door to try to figure out what it is. But a screeching makes her jump back – a high and breathy 'waaaah' that she's heard before though not for a while. It comes again and her brain crackles as neurons and synapses fire. Another screech and Mister barks at the door.

'No,' she says, looking at him. 'Can't be.'

A screech and the clinking grows frantic before falling to silence once more.

She lifts the card and stares at it, at the keypad – its red light lasering out into the corridor.

I don't want you to go in here.

'No,' she says, moving away and starting to walk back up the corridor. Mister doesn't follow. 'We shouldn't.' Another screech and he barks, looking up at her then at the door. 'Fuck.' She goes back, stares at the pad, the red light pulling her hand towards it – it has all the gravity of a black hole. 'He doesn't want us to go in here, lad.' More metallic clinking and he barks again. 'Fuck,' she says again. 'It can't be her, Mister… he wouldn't lock her up like this… not without telling us.' She sighs, looks up at the ceiling, then back at the red light. She glances down at the card and then lifts it, placing it in front of the pad until the light blips to green. Shhhhhh. The lock slides out of hold. She grabs the handle and opens the door before it has a chance to re-lock. Mister moves between her legs and puts his snout through the gap, sniffing. He pushes forward, forcing the door to open wider. She takes a deep breath and steps inside. White. White. There is white everywhere, except for lines of black in one corner. Some kind of movement behind them.

Another 'waaaah' and Mel blinks, refocuses. A white room, white shelves, white objects on them. The black bars of a cage in one corner. A creature behind them – beige and speckled.

'Teddy,' she says.

The bird tries to open her wings but her cage is too small – there is hardly any room for her to move. She tries to fly, clatters against the bars. A gold ring around the bottom of

Teddy's leg clinks against the metal – that is what was making the sound last night, earlier. Metal against metal. It makes her head ache.

'Jesus.'

She goes over to the cage. Teddy opens her beak, showing the pink inside of her mouth, but doesn't screech. Mel peers through the bars at the small bodies of creatures – voles, shrews – that lie in a huddle on a small shelf; small, black pellets the size of thumbs scattered across the floor of the cage. Streaks of white spattered down the perch and shelf.

Mister is up on his back legs and sniffing in Teddy's direction but doesn't bark. She turns away for a moment, takes in the rest of the room – the small, white objects on the shelves. The small, white objects that her brain thought were ornaments at first, but now she realises aren't. She moves closer to them – the strangeness of white objects on white shelves, like some kind of art installation. She peers at them – some with bulbous ends, others long and straight or short and stubby. They are grouped in such a way that similar sized ones are placed together, long and thin, short and nubbed; small ones clustered together like handfuls of pale pebbles. But no – she realises as she stares at them – they are not ceramic or plastic or anything like that. They are bone. Human bone. Human bones and teeth. Laid out like it's an exhibition.

An electrical whine and she turns away, in the direction it's coming from: up near the ceiling, where the two walls meet. A camera. Its eye full on her. Watching.

'Shit,' she says, her heart seizing. 'Come on… we need…'

To go. But the words don't come. She starts walking towards the door, clicking her fingers for Mister to follow. A clinking stops her. Teddy. She can't leave her in the cage like that. Trapped. Unable to stretch her wings. Constrained for however long before B returns.

She goes back, looks over the cage. Finds the door, the small loop of metal that is keeping it latched. She lifts it, the cage door loose but not open.

'I hoped you were going to be different.' B's voice from behind her then. 'Not another of *these*.' She turns as he glances towards the shelves, the clusters of tooth and bone there. 'But I guess I was wrong.'

B is in the doorway, in a blue suit, white shirt open at the neck. A long, gold chain hanging out of it now with something dangling from the bottom of it. Not on the way to the US but there, right in front of her – blue-black hair gleaming in the bright white of the room.

'B, I...'

He shakes his head. 'I asked you not to come in here... asked you, expected you not to...or–'

'Ordered me?'

'It's *my* house, so yeah, if you want to call it that.'

'There were noises... Teddy...I...'

'Teddy nothing. She was fine.' He takes in what she's wearing – the white t-shirt, the burgundy dungarees. 'And the blue disappears as soon as I disappear too, does it?' A bitter smile appears and fades. He shakes his head.

She glances down at her clothes. 'What are you talking about?'

'So much for being my good girl.'

'That's ridiculous. You're being ridiculous.'

A small gap in the door. She tightens her fists, moves towards it. But before she can get there, his hand is around her neck, pushing her into the cold of the wall, fingers squeezing. The gold around his neck blinks in the light.

Not a pendant at the bottom of it, as she'd thought, but five gold rings – all different: one with an emerald, two with diamonds, one plain, the other a band of gold leaves. He sees her looking at it, glances down. 'One for each of them,' he says, then looks at her own hand, at the small ring like a twist of gold rope around her little finger. 'I didn't think I'd be getting a sixth one though.' He tuts. 'Disappointing.'

She grabs at his wrists, lungs starting to seize, but can't loosen his grip. Mister is barking – a blur of brown at the bottom of her vision – then growling.

B grimaces, lets go for a moment. She gasps for breath. Mister's mouth is around the bottom of B's trousers, tugging, tugging, trying to get him off. B swings his leg backward then forward, swiping Mister along the tiles and out through the door. He pulls the door closed, hard – Mister locked out now and barking. Then B is back, grabbing for her neck again and pushing her slowly against the wall.

'I'm sorry I lied about the US,' he says. 'I just needed to see what you'd do… if you'd listen to me… or not.'

'Testing me,' she says with the croak of a voice.

'If you like.' He squeezes tighter.

She tries to gasp but the air won't come. The whiteness of the room flickers and begins to grey out at the edges of her vision. A metallic clanking. She tries to look over towards where it's coming from, to where there is a small, speckled body moving behind the black bars of the cage. Wings opening and pushing against the unlatched door, which now swings wide.

Mister barks, scratches at the door. Teddy screeches, as she emerges from the cage now – her wings flapping as if to get some blood into them. B keeps pushing, squeezing. Not seeing how Teddy dips low and then how she pushes herself up from the base, flying to the ceiling, towards the camera, the door, then back towards the cage. Mel blinks to try and get rid of the grey that is almost everywhere now but she can't. She is going, going, starting to fade.

Teddy hovers near the ceiling, the heart of her face in their direction, her eyes on them. Then she is flying towards them, hovering above. Head dipping, legs pushing forward until the sharp talons are almost touching B's head.

There is a wet sound, a ripping red that spurts across Mel's vision. B lets go of her, wafts his hands above his head as if to swat something. But the ripping continues. The talons gouging lines into the top of his skull, his face, his eyes, the side of his neck.

As Mel falls back against the wall, the greyness brightens to white. B tries to wipe the sight back into his eyes, the blood back into his body but too much of it is gone. He stumbles forward, spreading red across the white shelves and walls. Small feathers falling and catching in his hair.

'Good girl,' says Mel, when she is able to speak, when her lungs have filled with air once more. 'Good girl, Teddy.'

B is against the door, on his knees, red hands slipping down the white. Teddy circles the ceiling once more before descending towards the edge of a shelf, a splay of finger bones rattling as she lands. She is watching B as he slips further down towards the floor, towards stillness – dark eyes blinking. The heart of her face is streaked with red, her pink mouth open wide at the centre of it. But there is no sound, no screech, no breathy 'waaaah'. There is just the electrical hum of the camera above the door, its blind eye recording what is happening. The light click of metal against wood as Teddy lowers her ringed foot to the shelf.

Birthday

You have already blown out the candles, already opened your cards and presents, already heard 'Happy Birthday' more times than you are able to remember. You are ten. You are a big girl, bigger than you've ever been now that you've reached double digits. You have officially been ten since half past nine this morning – the time your mother gave birth to you ten years ago. In a hospital that is now boarded up, with paint peeling from its walls and radiators, and with 'Keep out' signs stuck to the barriers outside of it. You know about this because you've driven past with your family many times before and, so far, each time you have, your mother has said, 'Worst night of my life in there. But you were worth it. In the end.'

You are sitting at the dining room table which is spread with colouring books, yellow bricks of Lego, with felt tips that have lost their tops. You can see the dots and lines left by the felt tips all over its surface – the yellows, blues and pinks which are starting to fade now that you don't use them so much, now that your mother has scrubbed the life from them to try and get rid. But you can still see them, like scars. Like the table is holding on to the memory of you and your brother. As if it doesn't quite want to let your child selves go yet. As if it's not quite ready to just be a place for the eating of sensible meals.

You are at the dining table but you are not eating at home today. You are waiting for your parents and your brother to come back downstairs so you can all go to Pizza Hut for lunch, then ten pin bowling. It was your brother's choice to do this. You wanted Burger King and the cinema but your parents talked you out of it because your brother can't sit still for ten minutes and you've already had burgers this week. You said something about it being *your* birthday not his and your mother tutted. You heard the sound of that tut like a gun going off. Like a bullet fired in the room and you the only person who could hear it. A bullet that was nothing like all those you've heard fired in films before because this sound was louder – so loud and hard that it was as if no other sounds existed, or had ever existed. Like it was the first real sound you'd heard. It was as if it had the power of making the whole world quiet, quieter than it has ever been before. And now you can't stop hearing it. Or feeling the emptying that came with it. A feeling like all the colours you've been drawn in are draining away from inside you and you're not sure how to stop them leaving.

You know now what it means when someone asks you on your birthday morning – as your father did today – if you feel any different, any older. You know now that you shouldn't have been so quick to answer him with your bright and perky 'No' and that you should have waited until later. Until the time when your mother tutted. Until the time when you felt your colours start to go. If he asked you now you would probably get hot in your face and feel the water come to your eyes, and he would ask you why you were crying on your special day. He would rub you on the top of your head and say, 'Come on, what's wrong? You're a big girl now. Don't be getting upset.' And you would move your fists over your eyes and not be able to speak because that's what happens when you cry. A drawbridge goes up in your throat and there's nothing you can do to make it open again.

But you are not crying. You are sitting at the dining table staring at a red felt-tip scar in your new birthday clothes with your new birthday bra beneath them. Small ponies riding over the cups, small girls sitting tall on minute saddles laid over the ponies' brown backs. You won't need bras for another year or so but you've started to wear them now because you have two small lumps growing there. Hard as knuckles. Two hard lumps that will one day stretch and fatten until they start to look like your mother's. Soft and full and shaped like teardrops. But that won't happen for a while yet. For now you just have these rope-knots of flesh that your brother has taken to punching you in when you fight. Distracting you by aiming at your head with his fists and then lowering them at the last minute so he can hit them full on, right on the pink of their soft, puckered tips. The pain going through you in a liquid bruise. A squirt of flame that makes your vision pop with stars and your knees crumple like a house of cards. You have to give in to the crumpling and sit down when he does this. You have to sit down, lean forward and hold a hand over each small mound until the stars and heat begin to fade. And when they do, you get up and chase him all over the house until you catch him and kick him down there, hard as you dare. And when he howls, which he always does whenever you touch him, you know you're going to get it. You know you're going to feel that sting on your legs or backside while he just gets a good talking to. All because you're the big girl and you should know better, especially now that you're ten, especially now that you wear bras and have been able to colour inside the lines for a long time now, unlike your brother.

But you know he won't do any of this today, because of Pizza Hut and bowling. He won't hit you until you've at least got home again when your birthday day is drawing to a close. When it is becoming less than it was. When the day is narrowing and closing like an eye ready for sleep.

But the eye of your birthday day is still wide open. There are many hours to go before it is time for your brother to go to bed and an hour later, you. Before then you are going to drive by the hospital on your way to the restaurant. Your mother is going to turn in the car and say, 'Worst night of my life...' And you will want to ask her why, when she says this, you feel like you're the one to blame for all of what happened there. For the rips and the stitches. The blood loss. For the hot, sore weeks which almost made her not want to try again, try for her boy, the boy she had always known she wanted since she herself was ten.

But you won't ask that. Not when they've bought you games and clothes and earrings the colour of cuckoo eggs. Not when they came in singing with a cake in the shape of a horse's head, ten candles down its mane. Not when it said your name in a smiling curve on the cake board in front of it – a small star cut out in the 'a' so that it could become the dot of the 'i'. The icing ragged where the cut wasn't clean.

Instead you will hear those words again and say nothing. Your father will carry on driving, your mother will put her head back against the seat and your brother will play a game on your mother's mobile phone. You will stare at the 'Keep out' signs, at the one which is half-fallen from the mesh. You will breathe on the window, write 'No admittance' in the mist, spell it right. And you will feel again that same feeling from earlier, from when your mother tutted. Your reds and yellows slipping out through the horse-hair gap under the car door and out onto the road. Settling in rainbows in the puddles next to the kerb. Rainbows that bring their own kind of rain. The kind of rain that will never stop.

Mirrors

1

i wake
to metal mouth, a wetness all around it
me on the dusty floor
all heat and dry and burn inside
my stomach roils and rips with a hunger i don't recognise
          Pappa, I shout with my husk of a throat but no answer comes
          Pappa, louder, but still no answer
the curtains are shut even though it must be morning
                              or later perhaps from how high the sun is through the fabric
          burn burn
i cannot look for long   at the round yellow
the hot disc of light
          the way it stings and seethes and sears at my eyes
                    i turn away   lift my hand to wipe the wet from my mouth, then cover my eyes
but the wet has left blood on my fingers   from the metal taste at my lips
          i move my tongue over gums, around the inside of my cheeks
but cannot find the source of it
                                        Pappa, Pappa   but
my voice is a croak
                    my throat the dry of something dead

he could be out in his workshed
working at his mirrors
the way he has done
since being a boy
when his own parents lived here
but he would not have left me
lying here, would have opened the curtains
which are billowing out now
into the room
something on them that was not
there before though
a streak of red at the hem a scrunching in the
cotton as if someone has grabbed them
not my pappa though not my…
a gripe of ice and
i turn and crawl towards my bedroom
to find shadow, the darkness beneath the
bed to lie to sleep
to find a place where i can wish this strange fever
away
hour 1 hour 1
some voice inside me says
hour 1 of what? of?
i want my pappa here
to lift me
hold me and
make me full well
but now, now
more than anything else
i want i want to sleep and

for this sharp twisting
that is twining
and winding
inside of me
to go to
go to
go

8

Pappa has a thing for mirrors
not just making them, but seeing them
everywhere like certain numbers
he calls mirror numbers
1 8 11 88 101 111 181…
tetradic, their name is
numbers that stay the same no matter whether
they're flipped one way or another,
up
down
back front
or if a mirror
is used to split them in ha lf

he has made mirrors for years
his father's trade becoming his own as he
grew
so much so that for
miles around, this is where
people would come if they needed a new one,
for whatever reason –
if they wanted to smooth their skirts
before new squares of silvery glass

or if the men desired to know how
they looked with
their wiry scraggles of
beard or moustache

there is a scuffling outside now and
i crawl out from under the bed,
go back to the living room
to where the sun is
below the windowsill, the horizon,
the light dust-filled and grey the motes lit
up in rainbows of colour, like i have
never seen before
it must be
early evening or so now
around hour 8 of this fever an
hour which has brought with it
a fiery thirst the strangest of
hungers

another scuffle and i turn to find
shadowy flickers in the gap
beneath the front door,
the smell of something which could be
feast or foul or flower
what is it? and why does it
make my tongue come alive?
i move slow towards the door
to where there is
the thump of small feet, fast away
who is it and where are they running to?

                                        i touch the handle and
twist
peep out into the grit of this gloaming
                                        a boy – my schoolfriend
caleb – i know it is him because of
                    his smell   (his smell?)
running hard,
          elbows pushing back, school shoes kicking up dust
from the open ground

    smaller, smaller now until he is gone
                              home again   the
door shut hard behind him
as if he was feared for
          there is a blooming   – iron   sweet
fumes   which flower up
                        and make the griping in me soften
i look down   to where the smell is coming from
                                                  a jar on the
ground
                    and a velvet red inside it
so thick it clings to
the glass,   the liquid pulsing
with such a light
                    that this fever makes it hard for me to take
          my eyes from it

i manage though and lower
them to the square of paper that sits beneath the jar
                              i glance up – quick as a kitten –
and a curtain flickers at caleb's house
is somebody watching?

watching for what?
i take in the red
again, the square of white beneath it
then i fast-grab them, shut the door
behind me
sit with
them on the chair as dust
swirls in
the hearth

drink this the paper says in a scrawl of pencil
we will bring more
your pappa is dead
please don't hurt us
but i don't know what any of this
means
i have a fever
perhaps my pappa has gone
for a doctor he can't be dead
why would i hurt them?
the red in the jar blooms stronger
it is syrup and
sugar and something i cannot name
drink this the note says
drink this
but i
put the jar on the floor

and push it away from me
as the moon the moon the moon
crescents into view

11

midnight an aching
this fever and a knifing inside
this red may be medicine
but how am i to know if it is or not?
perhaps, if my pappa is
dead, i would die too if i did not take it
perhaps caleb and his family know this somehow
and they are trying
to help me
drink this drink this the note says
i wait and wait but
eventually the spiking is so strong
that i lift the jar and sip from it

LIFE LIGHT AWAKE GIVE OPEN
BLOSSOM SHINE

the jar is empty
the fever gone, fast as a falcon
i am myself again
more than myself perhaps
more than i was

there is a quietening inside me
a slow river of thinking in my mind
i push my tongue into the jar and lick it clean

when i finish i take it to the sink
wash it under the tap
then i put on shoes and go out to walk
beneath that fattening moon

the light out here makes my skin shine
it puts sparks in my brain such that it cracks
and crackles with a fast and beautiful fire

i do not feel like the girl i was
i am not sure i am her anymore

88

we saw it come from the woods
taking and tasting him
there was no hope – he was gone
and now it knows we're here
it might come back for the rest of us

a low voice wakes me at sunrise,
just as i have laid down to sleep
it is caleb speaking through the thin gap around my window
a trembling like ribbon at the edges of his voice

it is 88 hours, three days or so, since pappa left, since the
fever, since that first jar of medicine was left at my door
there has been much night-time walking since,
as well as sleeping in the daytime when my
energy flags – and there is an icy sharpness
in my mouth that was never there before

they all say you're the same as it now
but i tell them you're not – that's
why i bring the jars… because
no-one else will, but i know
you're still ok and
that you're still
our friend and
that you
won't
hurt,
you
–

and then he is gone

101

sleep and then sundown
i wake to flashes – like moon in a mirror
and the memories of what happened
before the fever return

my pappa his workshed locking up
walking back in blackness
something there a quick catching
but pappa gets away
shuts the door blood on his neck, on his clothes,
on his fingers but it's there
at the window peering in pappa grabs at the latch,
the curtain a screaming
a screaming that is coming from me
he is pulled out, taken and

before long it is back then back then
coming again for me
it bends and bites me
drinks me as it makes me drink it
i fade as the mirrored pendant at my neck
falls out of my nightclothes
the one my father made me
a circle of silver, shining shining out
it touches the once-man's skin, the pale of his hand
until there's a hotness, a hissing
the smell of foul
and i am dropped to the floor discarded
the once-man gone and going out
through the window
my pappa in his arms then, as he
takes him with him, back to the woods

111

i know how to help them – although in helping them i know
i will not be helping myself

caleb, i whisper to him through the wall of his house,
my voice a smelling salt that rouses him

wake, i tell him, *wake and listen*

he pulls his bedroom curtain to the side and blinks at me from the window
the day not yet here, but already the sleep gone from his eyes

the workshed, i say, *the pieces of glass*

you can use them to make what you need

i tell him about
silver nitrate,
sodium hydroxide
ammonia
sugar
how to use them, mix them
until they become the thing
that will help keep all of the village safe

later, as i sleep i smell mineral and metal
sense mixing and making
as memories flash at the edges
of my dreams

181

by dusk it was done

the villagers worked at the mirrors
until they had enough to hang them
from their homes   or shard
them into the ground all around
the village, and at the edges
of it too

enough enough of them now to keep
the once-man away, to scatter him
to the winds

808

over a month later now and the once-man has never returned
he has been shooed from this place,
sent away
although perhaps all we've done is shoo him somewhere else
to seize and sup the blood of others
others who may not think to use
mirrors against him – in the way that we did

i still walk at night beneath new moons, old moons,
drinking in colours i've never known before
rainbows that are violently alive,
blues and blacks so bright they could blind you –
heartbeats that i can hear from a hundred miles away

i just have to take care where i wander
so i don't catch myself on a mirror,
or *in* one either – it is strange to gaze at silvered glass
and to not see yourself looking back from it
nobody would know the black hole it creates inside of you
– an absence of sorts, where once something lived…
it is the same, i imagine, as losing your shadow

caleb is not the only one who brings me the jars
of animal blood now
everyone else does too
they don't just leave them at the door either –
they knock and smile
and ask me how i am
bring me flowers from the meadows beyond the mirrors,
the meadows i can no longer get to without risk to myself

they even take them down from outside the hut every week
so that i can enter it, play games, be part of village life again
they want me to feel that i am as i was
even though i know at the core of me i am not

it is not so bad a life though – if you can call it that
i have all that i need here,
caleb, a home,
a place that knows my depths as well as my darknesses
        and the other   the other   the other thing too
                i will always have this
                        the moon, the night
                                the smells it gives me
                                    the scent of blood
                                        on the breeze

Harbour lights

Some nights Didier dreams he is at Harbour Lights again. Moving through the sea of tables and chairs as fluidly as an eel, teeming plates of golden fish and chips in his hands, some balanced on his forearms like one of the circus performers he might have seen as a small boy on a day trip into Paris with his father. His father is long dead now. He struggles to recall his face sometimes, on those evenings when he thinks of him – when the light is low, when there is no television. When he is not thinking of the woman for the briefest time; the woman who brought him here to the grey Yorkshire coast, who steered him away from France and his father, the woman who has now also, somehow, steered herself away from him.

And always in these dreams of his, there is that feeling – that small rise and swell of fear – that one of the plates will unbalance and tip away from him towards the floor. The crockery smashing against the white tiling, the batter breaking open until the pale flesh of the haddock spills out. And the thought comes to him then that he will reach to save the falling plate but in doing so will lose all the others he holds. But there is only ever the threat of ruin; no plate ever falls to the floor. Even so, the dreams trouble him. And Didier wakes afterwards with damp in his palms and over his forehead. The arm that held the trembling plate trapped beneath the bulk of his belly, half-dead and tingling from the weight of him. He always turns onto his back then and massages it until the feeling returns, in the way she would have done if she were there. Pushing her fingertips into his skin, kneading and pressing, then perhaps kissing the crook of his elbow when it was alright again, when the blood was flowing into it once more.

*

It has been two months since he stopped working at the restaurant. Two months of sitting in the living room. Two months of forcing himself out to walk the town while avoiding the pier that he would often walk with her; sometimes returning to sit in her car to inhale the salt smell of her, turning over the engine from time to time but never able to make himself drive it. Two months of low appetite and broken sleep. Sometimes, he makes himself a hot chocolate for breakfast, in the hopes it will waken his tastebuds but it doesn't and he can only manage a few sips before pouring the chocolate away down the sink; the dark brown pooling around the plughole before draining away.

'Tartare sauce? Ketchup? Bread and butter?' Sometimes he catches himself saying the words out loud. The words he always said to diners as he delivered their plates of steaming food. Sometimes they would say no or yes to one or all. And he would bring the bread or the sauces before eventually leaving them with their cod or their haddock or their sole, saying to them, 'Enjoy your dinner', never 'Bon appétit', even though some of them might have expected him to, if they had noticed his accent or thought, as she did, that he looked just like a typical Frenchman.

'You just need a beret and a string of onions,' she'd laughed early on, teasing him for his combed black hair and moustache, his dark Gallic eyes. 'If I buy you a stripy top will you wear it?'

'No,' he'd said and pulled her to the bed, a hand to her hip. 'Absolument pas.' But, still, she had bought him one – blue lines on it the colour of the English Channel – and, yes, he had worn it for her in the way he never would have for anyone else. And now, all these years later, he wears it for her still.

*

'Tu es sûr?' his father had asked Didier on the morning almost twenty years ago now when he was to leave for England, for the woman waiting for him there. 'Are you sure this is what you want?'

Didier had gripped the handle of the small case resting in his lap and turned to his father, trying not to see the deep lines at the sides of his mouth, the mass of grey bristles over his face and neck. 'Yes,' he said. 'I am.'

His father had nodded, not taking his eyes from the backs of his hands on the steering wheel. 'You hardly know her… but it's your life and you're old enough I suppose… you're not a child. Not anymore.'

Didier had shook his head a little. 'No,' he'd said, thinking of the woman again – how she had looked that first time he saw her, at the farm door just a few weeks before: the shorts, the muddied boots, the backpack dropped at her feet; the velvet sound of her voice as she asked for milk and a place to sleep for the night, her grey eyes on his as she reached for the right words and the right way to say them to him.

Didier had tried not to stare at her, tried to breathe the heat out of his face. Then, when he showed her in and poured a glass of milk, he tried not to let her see how his hand shook. But it was pointless to try and hide anything from her. Those grey eyes saw everything. He could tell from the way she smiled as she took the glass of milk and drank it without looking away from him. And he could tell again days later as he moved over her in the spare room, when she held him and touched his cheek after, when he knew that she had seen into him and realised that she had been his first. Those eyes of hers didn't miss a thing.

'I'll come and visit,' Didier said to his father before climbing out of the pickup to go and get his boat. 'And you can always come to England and…' He half moved his hand towards him but was unable to make it go any further. The sad lump at his father's throat stopped him from doing or saying anything more.

His father nodded, glanced at him briefly then reached for the key in the ignition.

'Goodbye, Father.'

But his father did not take his eyes from the windscreen. 'I hope you'll be happy there.'

And Didier nodded before getting out and walking towards his ferry, turning back to wave at him before he went inside. But his father was no longer there: his pickup was already shrinking on its journey back to the farm and away from him.

It was nine months later when Didier and the woman were woken during the night by a phone call from one of the neighbouring farms. The man – Fabrice – telling him how his father had managed to drive to him before his heart had closed finally like a fist. Didier listened without saying anything then hung up, the woman holding onto him as if to stop him from falling to the floor. It was days before he was able to speak, months before he was able to accept that he would never see his father alive again.

*

The two of them had tried for a child. It was what they wanted and it seemed the right thing after such a loss as that. Girl or boy, they would name it for Didier's father: Jean or Jeanne. It would have her features and Didier's colouring, it would be taught to speak both languages from infancy. And it would have a happy life – that was certain. The child would be more loved than it was possible to be and by parents who themselves loved each other.

They would joke about this child that would one day sigh and roll its eyes at them, that would tut when they were too caring or protective. But it was clear to them: they would love it with full and open hearts and it would come before anything and everything else in their lives. The child would be blessed to have them and they would be blessed to have it. Fatherhood – never even a consideration for Didier while he was with his father on the farm – was here now, bright and promising as a moon. Brought to him by this woman who had backpacked around his country until she walked up the lane towards his farm and found him.

If someone opened him up and looked inside him he was sure they would see fireworks and sparklers there instead of lungs and a heart. That was how being with the woman made him feel, that was what the thought of having a child with her did to him.

Each month, though, the blood would come. And the woman would go into the bathroom after feeling the small, wet bloom of it arrive in her underwear. Emerging afterwards with just a smile or a shrug after the first few times, resignation and paleness when the months turned to years. The small, white sticks she had bought remained in their packets in the bathroom cabinet. But after five years of trying, Didier watched from the doorway as she took them out one by one and dropped them into a binbag; touching her on her arm as she passed him on her way to take the bag out to the bin in the yard. The talk of children at an end. Never to be mentioned again.

They never found out what their own particular reasons for childlessness were. Didier offered to go for tests while they were still trying and once even suggested that she might want to try and find another man instead – one who could give her what she wanted. But she had taken both of his hands in hers and kissed the backs of them, her grey eyes wide when she looked up at him once more. 'No,' she'd said. 'There is no other man.' And heat had flooded his eyes and chest as he nodded at her, a light trembling at his lip. And he knew then that he would never need to imagine a time when the woman would not be there with him, when she would not want to be in his life.

*

It was ten years into their time together that Didier woke in the night to the sound of the woman breathing raggedly beside him in sleep, as if sobbing. He touched her and she quietened before turning onto her back, her breath slowing and deepening once more. In the morning, he asked her what she had been dreaming about but she said she didn't know at first. 'I do remember a fishing boat though,' she added, holding the mug of tea to her chest as if trying to warm herself with it. 'It was night and it was coming into harbour, but all its lights were out – and the harbour lights too. I was on the pier… I could only just make it out. But its engine,' she said, clenching her jaw. 'I remember now… its engine was so loud that it frightened me. I thought my ears were going to burst.' She stared over towards the window but there was a glassiness in her eyes as if she wasn't seeing it at all. 'I thought it was going to come straight at me and crash into the pier. I remember thinking I just wanted a light to come on somewhere so I could see… but there was nothing but dark and the sound of that engine. I hope I never hear a sound like that again.'

*

The woman had to lie inside a machine when she found the first lump, a few weeks after the dream. Didier held her hand before she went in, told her that everything was going to be alright. He hoped that saying it would make it true. But when he saw her afterwards, there were dark dips beneath her eyes, a pallid look to her skin. She no longer seemed to be the woman she always had been, as if something had become lost inside her.

'In there,' she said, unable to finish her sentence. It was the first thing she had been able to say to him.

'Dis-moi.' He squeezed her hand but she did not squeeze back.

'It…' She swallowed. 'It sounded like that boat.'

'Boat?' he'd asked, not sure what she meant. He thought of the boats that slipped in and out of the harbour almost every day of the year but nothing would come.

'The one in my dream.'

He remembered what she had told him about the dream then – the low rumble of the boat, the lack of light. He told her again that she was going to be fine, that there was nothing to worry about but it was almost as if she wasn't able to hear him.

'Being in there was like being in the dark again on that pier.'

'They're going to help you, mon chou,' he said, cupping one of her hands with both of his. 'They're going to make you better.'

'It's like that banging's inside me now, that sound,' she said. She was staring towards a curtained window. 'It's like I'll never be able to get rid of it.'

Didier kissed the narrow valley that ran below her ear, between jaw and neck. He nuzzled his nose softly into it as if he was some kind of gentle animal. 'It's just a sound,' he said. 'Everything's going to be alright.'

She stroked the side of his face, slowly – her touch as cool as raindrops. 'I've always had a feeling something would happen, something out of the blue… at least now I know what that something is.'

*

Didier wakes now after another of the dreams at Harbour Lights. His hard, round belly heavy on his arm; his hand tingling once more. This time the woman was in the dream too – sitting at one of the tables: her back to him, hair tied in a bun, small wisps of curls resting against her neck. He tried to walk in her direction but before he could, one of the plates he was holding trembled and started to tip away from him; the fish and chips slipping on the porcelain until a light streak of grease trailed out from behind them. As he leaned to try and steady the plate, the others began to tremble too and it was as all of them began to tilt and fall away from him – in a way they never had before – that the woman moved her head in his direction. Didier's eyes opened though before she could see him, before he had chance to feel those grey eyes of hers on him one more time.

He wipes his forehead and glances at the clock: 22:01. He has only slept for fifteen minutes or so but is fully awake now. He knows there will be no more sleep for him tonight, not now that he has dreamed the woman back into his life again. He stands and goes to the window, lifts the curtain a little and glances out. There is a crescent moon hanging low in the sky, thin as a fingernail. He remembers the sight of the woman's hands, how they would look as they rested in his, how the tips of her own fingernails were as thin and white as that moon is now. He lets the curtain fall and starts to get dressed. He needs to go outside, needs to try and rid himself of the dream, the sensation of pressure that is there on his chest now, as if something heavy and winged has flown in and alighted there.

He leaves and steps out into the car park. He is halted by the sight of the woman's white car in their bay where she left it the last time she drove it, months ago now, to her last appointment. For a long time he has avoided looking at it, avoided trying to think about what to do with it. But there is something about the way the faint moonlight touches it now that makes him realise he will not be able to ignore it anymore. It looks otherworldly in this light, ghostly almost – as if it is not quite of this world or any other. If he touches it now, he is sure his hand will go through it as if through mist. That is how strange it looks in the night, how pale.

He takes his keys out and moves towards it. He places the key in the lock and opens the door, his heart thumping as he gets inside and reaches for the ignition. It will not start this time, he is sure of it. But he turns the key and the engine rumbles into life. His hand trembling as he takes the handbrake off and lets the car roll back out of the space. The brakes grinding, the creak of metal, but there is life in this car yet. It has not seized up as he thought it might have done after having been neglected for so long.

He pulls out of the car park then and drives through the dark streets of the town. He can see the blue blink of televisions through thin curtains, the warm glow of overhead lights and table lamps. He continues and before long realises he is driving towards the harbour and the small row of parking spaces huddled together not far from Harbour Lights and the pier. He pulls in and sits there for a time, the small orange lights on the dashboard greying out as he turns the key to off. He gets out and locks the door, lets his eyes wander towards the first few weatherbeaten planks of the pier – from where he and the woman would often start to watch for the comings and goings of boats.

'Didier!' a voice comes from behind him then. He turns. It is Derek, the owner of Harbour Lights – his jacket over his arm and car keys in his hand as he moves in Didier's direction. It must be ten-thirty – the usual time Derek leaves the restaurant when it has been a good night, when takings have been high and nothing untoward has happened in the kitchen.

'Ah, hello,' says Didier.

'How are you?' There is a warmth in Derek's voice and face that makes Didier's throat tighten a little.

'I'm fine… well, you know… yes, I'm alright.'

Derek squeezes the top of Didier's arm for a moment before letting go. 'We miss you,' he says, small sparkles of light in his eyes. 'You know you're welcome back any time… any time at all. If you ever want to that is.'

Didier nods and smoothes his fingers down his moustache. 'Yes,' he says. 'Thank you…'

'What have you been up to? Are you managing to get out? I haven't seen you for a long time…' He glances down towards Didier's shoes. Didier follows his gaze and sees what his old friend will also have seen, even in the dimness: that his left shoe is blue, the other black.

'Oh, I've just… you know… not been doing much,' says Didier, heat seeping into his face. But when he looks up again, Derek's eyes are no longer on his shoes but are passing over the car instead.

'Is that Maura's? I thought you might have…' But he doesn't finish his sentence.

Didier manages a nod. 'Yes… I thought I'd just take it for a drive…'

Derek continues looking at the car, his lips pressed tight together. His Adam's apple dips and he opens then closes his mouth as if unsure how to say something. 'It was cruel what happened,' he says finally. 'The way it took her like that. To think she was in the clear for so long and then… cruel.' He shakes his head.

Didier glances towards the pier. 'Yes,' he says, unable to say anything more.

'You loved her… she loved you – that much was obvious to anyone… we should all be so lucky to have something like that.'

A cloud the colour of ashes passes over the moon. Didier watches as it lengthens and thins before dispersing altogether.

'Don't let it ruin your life as well, Didier,' says Derek. 'Please… one life is enough…'

Derek puts his hand on Didier's shoulder before nodding, getting into his car and driving away towards his home on the edge of town.

Didier rests his hand against the cool edge of the car's roof, unsure what to do now – to get back in and go home again or to leave the car there and walk. A sound off in the dark of the water makes him lift up and walk towards it. It is a low sound yet, like a distant aeroplane. But it grows a little louder the further he walks and soon he is at the start of the pier, his stomach listing as he contemplates putting a foot onto it. It is like stepping out into an abyss, making that step onto the first plank after so long of not doing. The last time he walked it was with the woman. But he is on it now and moving forward, following that sound like a fish nosing through water. And before long he is up near the end of the pier, the water black and churning beyond it, the rumbling sound increasing although he cannot yet see where it is coming from.

He puts his hands onto the icy rail and peers into the night – the moon has slipped out of sight so not even the small amount of light from its crescent will help him to see now. The sound grows louder, reaching above the white noise hiss of the water. He moves his eyes in the direction he thinks it is coming from and can see something pale and moving in the air above the water now. He tightens his grip on the rail, a cold trickling down the back of his neck. It is like a small patch of glowing mist that is growing in size the nearer it comes. 'Maura,' the thought comes from somewhere. 'She is coming for me.' Even though he knows the mist is not the woman at all; still the sight of it makes goosebumps rise in a small, cold wave down the length of his spine.

The patch grows larger and the sound associated with it vibrates inside his body now. Whatever the light is, it is getting nearer. He thinks of returning to the car, of going home, but he cannot seem to take his hand from the rail. He carries on watching. There is a shape beneath the patch of light now; separating itself out from the blackness of the water. He tightens his hold on the rail and the shape draws nearer. An engine – that is what the sound is. And the shape, a boat: a late one coming in with its haul of plaice and haddock, its brown crab and scallops. Didier stares into the moving patch of mist above it and the shape becomes clearer: it is the pale bodies of gulls lit from below by the lights of the boat; the birds circling above it in the hope that they will be thrown something from the day's catch.

Didier takes his hand from the rail and breathes out. His lungs ache as if he has been holding his breath. The boat passes him on its way into the harbour. There are fishermen in orange waterproofs in the back of it, bending over as they sort through the slick mounds of fish and crustaceans. One of the younger ones is humming a tune that Didier doesn't recognise. A slow, mournful tune that makes him think of the woman, of the feel of her hand in his, the taste of her skin on his lips. Didier begins walking back down the pier, glancing in the direction of the woman's car as he does so but it no longer has the eerie look to it that it had before, not now that the moon has disappeared out of sight.

He hears a shout then from the boat and sees the younger fisherman standing now and lifting something up towards the gulls before throwing it at them. The fisherman stands there with his mouth open as a bird breaks away from the swirling group of them and dives for the food. It catches the piece of fish and is gone, away from the boat and into the shadows. The young fisherman laughs loud and long, claps his hands for a moment before bending and beginning to sort through the catch once more, starting up with his slow, sad humming again.

Didier is almost at the start of the pier now. A few more steps and he will be off the wooden planks and back on concrete. More steps still and he will be at the door of the woman's car and opening it up, driving away. He looks over towards the boat again, the boat that is beginning to slow and turn now as it pulls in for home. He can still see the young fisherman in the back, his eyes bright as he hums that unknown song while the night spins slow and certain above him. The young fisherman's hands move through the gleaming bodies of the fish that lie on the deck of the boat below him, slowly, carefully, in the same way they will on all the trips that are yet to come. Just as those hands that follow him will. On these same dark waters, under these same dark skies.

The Guide

Here he is, entering the cave. See how there is just a flickering of yellow light on the walls, moving with him as he steps further in to the cold blackness. This cave where the sun will never reach; this place which, without his light, would be too dark even for shadows.

He is slow so as not to snuff it out but when the leaf of flame he is holding thins and dims he stops and waits for it to build once more. Watching until the juniper wick fattens with light. Until the horse fat beneath it is slick and glistening with reflections.

You want to know how he's carrying the light? Well, by stone lamp, carved from red sandstone. See how it is shaped like a spoon with a handle and with a small bowl for the fuel. On the underside of the bowl, where you can't see, there's an engraving of an ibex. Its two horns curved as eyebrows. Just a suggestion of eye and nostril. A hint of jaw.

The ibex? It's an ancient goat.

Old goat? He is? Ah yes, a good joke. A very good joke indeed.

*

See, he is up to the wall now. His free hand touches it, feels its deep cold. There are many metres of rock beneath his palm. Such density keeps out the light and, therefore, the heat. But he has his skins to keep him warm. The skins of bison around his waist and shoulders, stitched together by needles made of sharpened bone. The beginnings of tailored clothing right there before us.

And now, as he crouches, he takes a roll of leather from his waist and unfurls it on the floor of the cave. I know the light is dim but squint a little and you can see our artist's tools: chunks of rock and charcoal, pouches of fresh bird droppings for his whites, iron oxides for the reds, brushes made with animal hair. The paints were made from minerals, burnt bone meal, charcoal mixed with water or blood, animal fats, tree sap. They were extremely inventive, you're right. Far more inventive than I'm sure we give them credit for.

But before he starts he will stand and hold his lamp to the paintings and drawings already there – the ones his father made before his sickness and which he will also make now and when his father leaves his body. Making this art is now his work, his role as part of his paleolithic clan. See how close he has to get to the wall, because the light is weak. But there, look, emerging from the rock the heads of four horses in profile and a lone horse with a red back and low, heavy belly. Bears, stags, mammoths, the occasional human in stick form. His father painted them all. As representations of the world beyond the cave, to appeal to the gods for good hunting? Who knows? Their meaning is lost to us now. We can only speculate about their intentions.

What is he going to draw? Patience, patience. Let's just watch and discover.

A clue? Good heavens. Alright. Perhaps it is something which is half-animal, half-human. I'm saying no more. You will just have to wait and see.

*

Look now.

He is beginning to draw a shape, holding the block of charcoal like a pencil. There is a rump, yes, curved, deer-like, but see how the legs end not in hooves but in feet, human feet. And how the head is the shape of a deer's but with human eyes, a human nose, human mouth. Unusual indeed, other-worldly. Next he dabs red onto its back to make it more real, to bring it to life. He will even spit the paint onto the rock or smudge it on with his fingers. He will be covered in it once he's finished, you're right. More paint on him than flesh. His very own artwork.

Then, beneath it, see, he draws a stick-human, slumped. Perhaps a representation of his father, the sick father I mentioned earlier. Perhaps he sees the creature above the human as one of their gods – a god he hopes will bring his father back to health. Make him the man he was again. But it's pointless, isn't it? The two of them have been dead for thousands of years already. Death will come for us all, regardless of our pleading or magic-making, won't it? But, yet, we try. We still try.

The way the stick-human's head is hung low makes me think of my own father, it's true. How he is now, in that place. A spool of saliva falling from his mouth, eyes to the floor, his brain no longer able to thread his thoughts together. He glances at me and gives me someone else's name. His brother's. He doesn't even know who I am so I have to play the part. I can no longer be who I am, his son.

Oh, I'm sorry, I'm sorry. I'm rambling. You don't want to hear this. You are not here to listen to me talk about myself. You're here for other things, more interesting things. You're here for the stories of these wonderful people with their intriguing ways and lives. Not me, not me. I promise I won't do it again.

*

Next he will do some hand paintings. All the while holding that stone lamp with its fading, flickering light so that he can see at least a small part of the rock, of what he paints. He's moved now – you can hardly make the creature on the stone out now, the stick-man. They have already been consumed by the blackness.

He takes the paint into his mouth, supping at it as if it's water, holding his hand to the wall and spitting at it, covering the rock and his hand in paint the colour of blood. But look – just the same as when you all used to paint around your hands when you were little – when he takes his hand away… ta-da! The shape of his hand is there surrounded by this rusty brew.

How do I know it was his father he drew earlier?

Well, I don't of course. It's just a theory. I know his father is ill and it seems sensible that he'd want to try and do something to make him well again. That's what any one of us would do.

How do I know his father is ill?

Well, I'm not sure I can answer that. 'I just do' doesn't seem adequate, does it? But he is. I know he is. I can sense it. Anyway, I shouldn't have allowed myself to meander off into all of that. That's not why we're here. We're here for the art, how it is made. Let's just concentrate on that. Well, we can try at least.

*

Look now. He takes the black paint into his mouth, places his hand just to the side and spits once more. This time when he removes it the shape is surrounded as if by shadow. The fingers and palm lying within a dark halo; blackness all around.

Is it symbolic of death?

It's a little threatening maybe, yes. But we are interpreting that from the time and place we are now; we can't possibly know what this painter intends, if he intends anything at all. Perhaps he just wants to see how his hand will look on the wall. Perhaps he's just curious.

Yes, you're right, his hands *are* large for his size. I've never noticed that before. Let me clean my glasses so I can see a little better. Yes, you're correct. In fact, they're somewhat reminiscent of my father's hands. He's not a big man either. Quite slight; bird-boned. But his hands! They're the hands of a giant. I used to put my own small hands up to his when I was a child, hoping they would be the same size – but they never were of course. Not even as a man, not even now on those odd occasions where I place my hand to his without his knowing. Mine is always the one within, shadowed by his. He could crush it if he so wished. But he hasn't become violent, not yet, not yet…

My father could have killed with those hands, but instead he chose to use the brushes and tools of the archaeologist. Digging and uncovering bones, gently dusting sand or dirt from cracked skulls or vertebrae. Yes, perhaps, from the long-buried bones of our painter here – who knows? But I digress once more. We're not here for my story. I don't know if I'm reminding you or reminding myself! Let's get back to our cave artist and see what else we can learn.

*

Now, see, before we leave, the painter returns to the half-human, half-animal creature he painted earlier, and, yes, the stick man. He is going to add to them. Smudge the white bird-droppings onto both bodies so that they're sharper, more defined. I'm not sure why he didn't do it before. He's obviously got an artistic eye – forever tinkering and improving what he's created.

No, I've already said, I'm not sure if this is meant to be a god and the man's sick father. I was just speculating. There's no way of knowing. There's no…

Now, remember, on your way out you can buy postcards of this painting. It will be a nice keepsake for you. Something to remind you of your visit. I have it myself. I placed it on my father's bedside table and propped it up against the base of the lamp so he can see it from his bed. It's strange to think of that lamp, that artificial light in my father's room, illuminating the postcard. While here we have one of the first lamps made by humans, a guttering stone lamp, barely illuminating the real thing. It's strange indeed. Like a link through time. But I ramble once more.

Any final questions?

No, I don't think that painted creature, if it was a god, had any powers that could bring his father back. That's highly unlikely. It didn't have any powers then and it doesn't have any now, I'm certain of that. I didn't buy the postcard for that reason, no. I am not so deluded as to believe that.

*

But now, as the painter leaves the cave with the dying light in his hand, let us also leave, and take with us what we have learned. Try to forget what I told you about the painter's father, or my father. You will learn nothing from any of that. Just think of the marks on the wall, the animals and the stick figures. How he spat the paints onto the rock, dabbed them with his makeshift brush. Those are the things you need to take from this. Not the other things. Just the man, his work, the cool spit of colour against the cave wall.

Table for one

The woman comes on Wednesdays. Seven-fifteen on the dot. Dressed to the nines in heeled boots and a thin blue scarf looped around her neck; the little silver speckles in it catching the light until it has the sparkle of river.

It has been this way for six weeks now, since she first appeared from nobody knows where. It was April, the same time as those late snows that had not been forecast. Standing in the doorway beside the 'Please wait here to be seated' sign; a crust of ice on the toes of her boots, hair glinting gold beneath the old chandelier. When Rudy walked over, all she said was, 'Table for one.' No hello, no thank you, no remarks about the weather. But with a softness to her voice. Rudy, always attuned to his customers, said nothing; just smiled and held out his hand towards the small, walnut table in the far corner, where the light from the chandelier only just reached. He pulled her chair out, took her order – wild mushroom ravioli shining with sage butter; a glass of oak-aged chardonnay – then left before returning with the wine, and later the pasta. Retreating quickly, in the way he sensed the woman wanted him to, saying nothing each time.

When he looked over ten minutes later though, the woman was not there. The scarf no longer hanging from the back of the chair, the food and the wine untouched. As he walked across, puzzled by the emptiness of the seat, the clean tablecloth, he half expected there to be no money either. But there was. Two new notes, fresh and clean as starched linen, lying next to the fork that had not been lifted once. More than enough to cover the bill, as well as a tip. He placed the cash in the till, the tip in the bowl behind the bar, all the while wondering what it was the woman had disliked – the food, the ambience at The Red Cat; perhaps, even, Rudy himself. But when he woke that night and turned everything over like a coin, he still wasn't sure. After a time, the woman eventually faded from his mind and he slept, falling into a dream of empty chairs that floated down rivers made of fabric in a glittering blue.

*

He was surprised, then, to see the woman return the following Wednesday, standing once more by the sign, in the same boots, the same scarf. 'Oh,' he said, 'hello again,' half expecting her to say something about a family emergency, having to leave. But there was nothing except, 'Table for one,' in the same way she had said it before. Her voice warm sand, glimmers of gold in her eyes and in the lightest strands of her hair.

Questions grew inside him – *Was everything alright, Madam? Was something the matter with your order?* – but he pushed them away, sensing once more that the woman only wanted to be seated and to tell him what she wanted. That time, she ordered salmon with anchovies and chicory, a white pinot noir. After he took the wine to her, then the fish, he watched from the other side of the restaurant; how she leaned forward, stared into the glass, then down at the food. Staying that way for a time before sitting back and running a finger across an eyebrow, then wiping her palms down the front of her skirt. Another minute or so and she stood, pushed her chair back, picked up her scarf and wrapped it around her neck. As Rudy started to walk towards her, he was called by another table – 'Can I have another knife, please? I've dropped…' – and so he was unable to say anything, to ask what the problem was. And by the time he delivered the knife, she was gone, although the money was there, same as before. More than enough to cover the bill as well as a healthy tip. He checked but there were no fingerprints on the glass, the cutlery was in the same place he'd laid it. It was as if the woman had never been there at all.

'Well, there's nothing wrong with what I sent out,' said Anton, the chef and co-owner of The Red Cat with Carlos, his friend.

'No, no,' said Rudy, scrunching the bottom of his cumin-coloured apron. 'Of course not. But it's strange, isn't it? How she comes and goes…'

'If she pays, I wouldn't worry,' said Magda, the wine curator. 'It's all about the money, isn't it?' She smirked then winked at her boss.

Anton pulled at his earlobe. 'No, it most certainly isn't.'

'Maybe I should try and talk to her…?' asked Rudy.

'No,' said Anton, his earlobe scarlet. 'You might scare her off altogether if you do that.'

'Seriously though, there might be something else going on.' The bracelet of tattooed stars around Magda's wrist shimmered as she wiped a glass. 'Maybe it's not about the food or the drink. Maybe she's here for something else.'

Rudy stared at her; the corner of Anton's lip twitched. But she flipped her red hair over her shoulder and turned away from them, without saying anything more.

*

It has been almost two months and still they do not know why the woman comes. Every time Rudy has thought about asking, the words have dried on his tongue like dead leaves.

Anton has always been too busy to get involved. Magda has just stayed behind the bar, shaking her head at him. 'No,' she will say, rubbing a fingertip over the coloured stars at her wrist. 'We'll either find out or we won't. It might just be something she needs to do.'

*

Tonight, the air in The Red Cat vibrates with electricity, so much so that Rudy's joints are alive with it. It is after seven – almost time for the woman to appear. Anton is ill with a fever and so Carlos is in the kitchen instead. These two changes, the electricity and Carlos, are the reason why Rudy has decided to steel himself and talk to the woman. 'Madam,' he will say. 'Is there anything we can do better?' Or, 'Is there something more you want from us?' He decides the right words will come to him in the moment he stands before her though. He will know what to say when she is here and seated at her table.

A sudden breeze and the door opens. The woman – blue scarf, heeled boots; the golden light from the dusty chandelier turning her hair to flame. Rudy turns away for a moment, notices Carlos in the doorway to the kitchen. Sees how his dark eyes travel down the woman's head and body until they stop at the pointed toes of her boots. He does this with curiosity, as if trying to understand the ways of a creature he has heard of but never encountered. There are knots between his eyebrows, a soft light in his eyes. Rudy has not had many dealings with Carlos before – being a fairly silent partner in the business – and has only met him a few times. He is entranced though; by the pure concentration in Carlos's face – a light beam focused through a prism. In that moment he remembers what Magda once said to him, that Carlos was from a family with 'gifts'. He had asked what she meant, but she just stroked her tattoo and stared at him. 'You know,' she said finally, eyes piercing into him. '*Gifts*. Like they have one foot in this world, one in another.' And she wiggled her fingers and widened her eyes at him but Rudy didn't have a clue what it was she was talking about.

'Hello, again,' Rudy says to the woman now. 'Table for one?'

She smiles and nods, but that is all. Follows him as he guides her over to the small table where the light from the chandelier barely reaches. He pulls out her chair, places the menu down. Takes out his pad and clears his throat, bones buzzing with the electricity that is all around and getting stronger now.

'Spatchcock chicken, please,' she says. 'And a glass of chenin blanc.'

He scribbles hard onto the pad, the pencil scratching a hole in the thin paper. He shakes his hand to try and calm it, writes once more – barely able to read his own handwriting. 'Very good,' he says, glancing up to find Carlos still in the doorway, his eyes continuing to take in the woman.

Rudy scratches his forehead with the rubber end of the pencil, clears his throat again. 'I…,' he says. The woman watches him. But he cannot think what to say. 'I…,' but nothing comes. At that moment, Carlos turns and retreats into the kitchen, the door swinging and coming to a rest in its frame. Rudy manages a smile, dabs at a patch of damp above his lip. 'I'll go and get those,' he says, the back of his neck prickling as he heads to Magda for the wine, then into Carlos where he will ask him to make the best spatchcock chicken he has ever made in his life.

*

Rudy's nerve fails him when he brings the woman her wine and knows it will fail him again when he delivers her food. There will be no revelations tonight, no discoveries about why the woman comes to The Red Cat every Wednesday. There will just be the usual untouched food and drink, the two notes on the table beside the fork, the woman walking out of the restaurant without saying another word.

The bell from the kitchen rings. There is a collapsing feeling inside Rudy's chest – a small sinkhole opening up under his sternum, pulling his hopes about the night into it. He goes through the swinging door and to the bench where the plates for service are placed. He studies the metal, then glances over at Carlos who is working on a fillet of beef. Rudy lifts the only plate that is there. Empty but for one thing: not a spatchcock chicken but a sprig of holly crafted out of icing. Leaves and berries but nothing more.

'Table two?'

Carlos lifts his head, nods at the plate in Rudy's hand then returns to the beef.

'What…?' He frowns down at the holly: the bright green of the leaves, the sharp points around their edges, the cluster of berries. 'It should be spatchcock. Where is it?'

Carlos raises his head once more, looks at the holly then up at Rudy. 'Did you know holly trees turn on genes to make their leaves spiky if they can sense they're being grazed on by animals?'

Rudy stares at him, unable to understand what Carlos is saying. 'What?'

Carlos smiles. 'I know. I didn't know that either. Amazing, isn't it? *They* told me.' And then he continues with the meat.

They? Rudy watches him but doesn't say anything else. Then he scratches his ear with the edge of his thumbnail, looks at the holly but doesn't know what he is supposed to do with it.

'Service,' says Carlos. 'Before it goes off.' Then he winks and nods at the door behind Rudy, smiling as he continues to slice.

Rudy shakes his head and carries the plate out into the restaurant, letting the door swing to a close behind him. He sighs down at the holly, tries to construct sentences that consist of apologies and explanations, but nothing comes together in the way he wants it to. He glances over at Magda who sees what he is carrying and begins rubbing her fingertips over the glowing ring of her tattoo.

He walks to table two, cheeks hot beneath the light from the chandelier. The woman is staring down at the glass of wine – untouched. She does not seem to hear him approach and so he clears his throat until she lifts her head, sits back. He places the plate down in front of her, prepares to say 'sorry' for what he is presenting her with, but the word fails to make it out past his throat. He readies himself for what is certain to come: a look of horror, a gasp, an outburst at such a ridiculous thing as this. He braces himself, tightens his hands into balls. He has never been shouted at in all his years as a waiter, not even when he served up gazpacho with a dying fly in the middle of it, moments after the insect had decided on an act of soupish suicide. Tonight is the end of his clean record though. Of that he is sure. After that perhaps he will never work at The Red Cat again.

The woman glances up, then down at the plate. She leans forward, pushes a finger towards the holly, lets it touch the points of a leaf. Looks up again. A sudden glassiness in her eyes, the light in them turning to water. She lifts the holly and the berries, places them in her palm, a fingertip touching the green then the red. 'I...,' she says, a trembling in her voice he hasn't heard before. 'Thank you.'

Rudy's mouth opens; his heart thumps beneath his ribcage.

'My daughter,' she says. 'Holly. She was training to be a chef. It was all she wanted to do. But she became ill... out of the blue. Then she... she... left me... on a Wednesday.' She places her other hand over the holly, cupping it in the dark cave of her palms. 'She said she'd let me know she was OK... that I'd know it was her.' She smiles. 'She loved cats, loved the name of this place... we always meant to come but... ah. I knew if she could talk to me in some way though, it would be here, through food.' Her cheeks are pink and shining bright now.

Rudy's throat tightens. There is something about the woman's voice, her face, the way she is holding the holly that is stopping him from speaking.

'I'm sorry I didn't eat anything. I just couldn't... without her.' She smiles at him then looks at the holly once more, pushes the chair back, stands. Rudy turns towards Magda and Carlos who are standing behind the bar, not smiling or speaking, just watching what is happening.

'Thank you,' the woman says. 'For everything. Truly.' Then she wraps the scarf around her neck and walks out, still softly holding the holly.

Rudy knows then she will not come back to The Red Cat again, now she's had her message. And so he watches her leave, the chandelier rocking at the sudden breeze through the door that she has opened, now closed. The golden light illuminating this table which is so often in the dark. Making everything on it bright and gleaming for a time: the cutlery, the glass, the white plate; the tablecloth which, tonight, is empty of money.

Mariposa

11:46 Harrogate to Leeds

Snow. Twenty minutes before your train is due. White fluff tumbling out of the sky and catching on your eyelashes.

'Don't like the look of this,' says one of the rail workers, staring up, fingers working hard at the ribbon of his lanyard. 'Wasn't even forecast.'

'No,' you say, as you straighten the straps of your rucksack, his eyes flickering in your direction.

He presses the plastic cover holding his photocard into the peach-like groove that separates his chin into two – one half more chubby than the other. 'Wouldn't surprise me if everything comes to a stop before too long.'

Better not, you think but don't say. What if you get stuck part-way? How will you get back then? It's not like your mother can come and get you if the snow's heavy. It's not like you can walk back all the way from Lancashire to Yorkshire. It would take you days.

The worker walks off towards where the driver is sticking his head out of a little window at the front of a train. The two of them nodding at each other then up at the sky before turning back once more. The worker moves away then and blows a whistle as the train doors shut. He lifts a hand to the conductor as the train pulls away, out of the station and into the white.

*

You are going to Preston for the girl.

That's the reason you're getting on a train in January in the snow – back over the Pennines to the city where you finished your degree last year. And where you decided never to go back to again, not even for graduation.

You haven't told your mother why you're going. Not really. You've said it's for the books that the girl borrowed from you and which you now need to get back, even though you're unlikely to ever read a book again. That part is true – about getting the books. She borrowed them from you, for extra reading on the module you both did in third year: Vampire Fictions. You'd come across three anthologies while browsing the charity shop near the university – two of stories, one of essays on the figure of the vampire. And you bought, but then never read them apart from one of the stories about a young, new vampire who used mirrors to keep her village safe from another more threatening one. You remember how poetic and strange the text was – the words splayed across the page as if someone had held them from a height and dropped them. It gave you a headache, made you not want to read more. Then, after the module started, and you and the girl got together, she browsed your shelves in boxers and a t-shirt, the pale red light from the bedside lamp making a creature of her. She saw then slid the three books out of their space above other books you hadn't read, placed them on the jeans she'd flung over your neatly folded clothes on the chair, tapped the backs of them.

'I'm having these,' she said. 'You're not gonna read them anyway, are ya? Slacker.'

There'd been a slight stumbling inside you at the way she raised her eyebrows, like she knew something about you that you didn't. Something about being all intention and dream, all fantasy. Little else. And the words your mother sometimes said to you came back to you then, though they were never said with cruelty – *you're a thinker, not a doer, love.* But the way the girl kept a finger to the books, the same way she'd kept a finger on your wrist after, made it all fall away. And so she took them. You feeling even then that you might never see the girl or your books again. And maybe you'd been right.

*

Your mother would have said you were an idiot for letting the girl take them. She would no doubt have said something else if she'd known the girl wasn't just a friend but that you'd slept with her. *I thought you'd have met a decent lad instead, Mari,* she might have said. *Don't turn out like him, for God's sake.* She'd be talking about your father, of course. *The sperm donor.* The man your mother had been involved with more than twenty years ago now, during a brief stint in Gran Canaria where she worked in restaurants and bars, first in the capital Las Palmas, then Puerto de Mogan and, finally, Maspalomas – the coastal town where she met your father.

You remember your mother telling you the first time she saw him, all brood and dark as he sat on his own at a table beneath an old, flickering streetlight outside *Casa Canaria,* drinking a bottle of beer with a sour twist to his lip. He ordered *papas arrugadas* and *mojo* – the Canarian specialty of wrinkly potatoes and spicy sauce – but when she brought them to him, he took a bite and spat them out, telling her they tasted like *mierda* because the potatoes needed more boiling, more salt, the sauce pale and bland – not fit for a Canarian to eat. *Back,* he had said, his voice almost a whisper. *Take back... please.* Somehow though – and you've never been sure why – this exchange eventually led to your mother giving him a glass of *ron miel* and him walking her home from the restaurant, along the nudist beach back to her apartment. People coupling in the dunes as they passed. A yellow moon, soft as butter, growing hazy in the hot air above and around them. He never spoke to her once on the walk; instead, she did the talking in her halting Spanish, telling him about England, its winters, the occasional flurries of snow there, which made his eyes widen. At least in your imagination. Then she kissed the honey rum from his lips beneath the broken light outside the apartment block, placed his hand on her hip. Your mother taking his fingers and leading him up the stairs then, his only words being how pale she was, even in the dark of her apartment. *Blanca*, you imagine him saying to her. *Tu piel es tan blanca.*

*

You have never known your father, wouldn't know him if you fell over him in the street. Jose-Maria, or Pepe as he was known. The man who only exists now as a figure in that single, faded photograph of him and your mother, the one you found buried at the bottom of a shoebox down on a shelf in the cellar. The only thing you're able to say for certain about him is he had dark hair and a heart-shaped face, the same as you have; that he was real enough to have been captured on film. But that is all. Your mother has given you very little over the years – just the restaurant, the walks along the beach, the hints of his voice. You have filled in the rest. You have no idea if he is still alive, still on that island, if he has other children, a partner he's soft with. If he ever wonders about you, or even knows anything about you at all.

You had told the girl all this after Vampire Fictions one day, before the books, before the kiss in your doorway, before you let her go down on you that first and only time she came to your room. You had fallen into step together after class, ended up walking to the refectory for coffee and doughnuts, both having an hour free before your next seminar – hers in English Lit, yours in Creative Writing.

'What's your name?' she asked. 'There's never a register, so…'

'Mari,' you said – still not sure even now if you flatten the 'a' because you're from Yorkshire or because that's how it would be pronounced in Spanish, by your father, your father's Canarian family, by those others from the islands.

'Unusual,' she said.

'Suppose,' you said, leaving your mouth open to say more but stopping, aware of a heat kindling in your cheeks and in the thin dip between your breasts.

'Hot.' Her eyes lingered on you as she bit into her chocolate doughnut, a pink hundred and thousand falling from her lip.

'It's …'

'Go on,' she said, licking the plump place it had fallen from as she waited for you to say more.

'It's Mari… short for Mariposa.'

'Oh?'

'Means butterfly in Spanish,' you shrugged. 'My mother used to live there… the Canary Islands. She liked it… the name I mean, so that's why… but everyone just calls me Mari… they never say the whole thing.'

Silence for a while, her eyes on you the whole time. 'I know how I could make you flutter,' she said eventually, a slow smile forming on her lips. 'Little butterfly.'

You looked down to the floor, aware of what she'd said, aware of how you'd been rambling and so you stopped before you told her what your father had said to your mother after she'd announced the pregnancy, when she'd told him the name she was thinking of if you turned out to be a girl. *Mariposa?* he'd said, eyes wider than your mother had ever seen them. *Mari… posa?* Your mother nodded, those butterflies of your name fluttering beneath her ribcage as she waited for a smile that never came. *Joder. No. That's what we call the queers here,* he said. *Little mariposas because of the way they flutter up and down with their stupid, fucking walks.* He lifted his hands at her, wafted them into short wings so weak they'd never be able to fly anywhere. *No kid of mine is going to be a fucking mariposa. Vale? Entiendes?* It was after days of silence that your father suggested calling you *Nieve* instead, the Spanish word for snow; something he said he wanted to see for real but probably never would because of the near African heat of the Canaries.

It was weeks after this that your mother walked home again through those same sand dunes she'd walked with your father, an orange moon blazing in a violet sky. She slipped in the shifting sands as she climbed an incline, clutching the small rise of her belly as she fell. Staying there and smiling as she rubbed the place where your small body moved for the first time, making her laugh as those butterflies took flight inside her again. This time for the quickening; that first movement of the baby in the mother's womb. She wanted to get back, tell your father all about it, but it was as she started to push herself up that she heard the noises from behind her, in a small dip in the dunes that was tufted by long, dry grasses. The light groan of a man followed by the low words of another. *Joder. Joder.* Something making her walk towards the sounds until she could see one man sitting there with his eyes closed, his head back against the soft wall of sand. Another man bent over him, head moving up and down, the orange light catching in the black of his hair. *Pepe,* she said, and the man lifted up, eyes widening as the other one turned away as if trying to disappear into the sand at his back. *Laura,* your father said, trying to move towards her but unable to because of the sand, because of the clothes tangled around his ankles. She ran through the dunes then to get away, get to her apartment. Covering her ears and ignoring the buzzer once inside; the buzzer that was pressed and pressed for an hour or so, then again for another hour just before dawn. Your mother telling you your father wouldn't want to press other buttons in case he woke the whole block up, which could lead to questions, raised eyebrows, accusations of all kinds. In the morning she packed her things and left by the fire exit, with a suitcase and a rucksack. Heading down the dusty backs of houses to get to the taxi rank in town, asking the only driver there to take her to the airport so she could get on the next flight out of there. Not once thinking of returning. Not for your father. Not for the island. Not even for you. On those nights when you begged her to, so you could go there to try and find him. Go and find your daddy.

*

12:57 Leeds to Preston – Delayed

You have made it on to your next train at Leeds but it isn't moving. It's just sitting on the platform as the minutes tick past the scheduled departure time; your rucksack on the seat next to you, a caramel latte on the table, growing cold. There has been no announcement but the snow is heavier now, the whole city glittery and white as you pulled into it. When you got off the Harrogate train and looked at the departure boards for Preston, you tried not to notice how many were showing as delayed or cancelled. At least ten of them. Yours – the one to the girl – one of the only ones still showing as being on time, even though it arrived two minutes late and hasn't moved a centimetre since. Ten minutes on and its engines are still silent.

You texted the girl about the books last week, about wanting them back, but didn't hear anything from her – not until yesterday. Your stomach fluttered as you opened her message. *If you really want them you'll have to come for them or you won't get them,* she had written. *Let me know when, just in case I'm doing someone else.* The fluttering became a heaviness somewhere in your abdomen until another text arrived a few seconds later: **something else* and a winking face with its tongue sticking out. *I'll come tomorrow,* you told her straight away. *Fine,* she wrote. *Meet you in 'spoons about one.* Not a question but a statement. One to which you replied, *cool, looking forward x,* but the girl sent nothing in response.

You have read over her texts dozens of times since then, trying to decide if there is more to them than you first thought. A macrocosm of meaning in the microcosm of text. She had a reputation for sleeping around at university, for being a dawg, so you weren't surprised when she ignored your messages, avoided you at university after having you – but now you're wondering if this wasn't because of you but something else. She'd sent a winking emoji after all so maybe she was still interested. Maybe something else had happened – a tragedy of some sort, a breakdown – that had knocked her out of whack, made her disappear? *You'll have to come for them or you won't get them...* maybe this was her way of getting you back near to her again, back in bed? There was a tingling below your abdomen at the thought of it, a whirling in the back of your head that almost made you feel faint. And she had corrected her text so you didn't think she was sleeping with someone else, hadn't she? Or were you just reading too much into things, as your mother has said to you many times before: *Mari, the reader into everything.*

You look out of the window at the two members of staff who are talking to each other, one of them shaking their head, the other glancing somewhere above the train. There is a mumbling further up the carriage and a man and woman stand, grab their bags from the overhead compartment and walk past you, heading off the train and out onto the platform. You glance around but nobody else moves so you open your rucksack to check you have everything: your purse and other essentials – as well as a few pairs of knickers, a small washbag, a fresh top. Just in case you stay. Just in case the girl wants you and you decide not to come back home. Ever again maybe.

A text from your mother then: *You shouldn't be travelling in this, Mari. You might get stranded x.* You don't reply. Instead you close the message and go back to looking at the girl's texts, reading them again to try and make them into what you want them to be: a declaration of sorts. *You'll have to come... You'll have to come.* The tingling grows stronger so you close the message, put the phone down on the table, take a sip of your caramel latte and wipe at your mouth.

You glance up at the screen next to the train – still 'delayed'. Nothing has changed; the engines still silent. The station workers are no longer standing there now though. There are just people gathered in front of the big departure boards, pointing or shaking their heads, sometimes dropping their bags to the floor. Some of them are checking their phones.

A man walks past your window then and for a moment he makes you think of your father – how he looks in the photograph: the black hair, the olive skin, the way he is turned slightly away, how he is squinting up towards the light. You watch as he heads from the train and towards the barriers, then imagine him going out of the station and into the snow. Standing and marvelling at the bright of it, the way it creaks and sparkles, how each snowflake merges with others until it becomes something bigger, something more.

You imagine your father in the sand dunes again then, with the other man, his head low and moving. You wonder if he ever managed to see the snow he wanted to see, whether he might still see it one day. If he ever leaves the Canaries to do just that. *Nieve.* The Spanish word for snow. A small whirlpool opens up inside you at the thought of him. How he hid in those dunes so that he could do what he wanted to. Be with a man. Be close to someone who was not your mother. Then how he was discovered. Running after her to try and make everything stop. To try and wipe what she'd seen from her eyes, her mind. Make everything OK.

Another text: your mother. *Let me know you're OK, will you? x.* Low voices on the train then, and movement, followed by the sound of footsteps along the carriage floor. A woman with a rounded belly shuffles past, sighing as she goes and pulling her coat tight around her. She can't fasten it properly because of the bump. It is too big. She goes out onto the platform and glances up at the screen, as you do now too through the window: *Leeds 12:57 Cancelled.* Others are standing in the carriage now, taking down bags, putting on coats. There are sighs and tuts, rumblings of complaint. And then an announcement: 'This is the train driver speaking. Unfortunately, this train has now been cancelled because of the weather. Please make your way out onto the platform and speak to a member of the station team who will be able to advise. Please remember to take all your belongings…'

You think of the girl and there is a crumpling inside, like leaves crushed in a hand. You stand, pick up your phone and rucksack and head out onto the platform. Stand beside the pregnant woman, both of you looking up at the screen, even though nothing has changed on it, or will change on it now. You glance down, taking in how the woman's hand is holding her belly, making the clothing and skin warm beneath it – the heat spreading down inside her until the baby that is growing there can feel it too. The whirlpool spins faster as you keep your eyes on her hand.

Your mother held her own hand to her belly as she fell on the dunes, just before she discovered your father. Had you felt that same warmth through her clothes and skin, down into the amniotic fluid around you, then into your own flesh? Colouring it with heat? *No kid of mine is going to be a fucking mariposa.* The sharpness of your father's words comes back to you then, makes you swallow. You put a hand to your throat for a moment, as if the words have pricked you there. You rub at the skin. Try to get rid of the feeling. Think again of your mother's swollen belly, the words that must have stabbed at the brightness inside her as she told your father the name she wanted for you. Then, how she packed her bags and ran through the streets to get away as fast as she could. Leaving your father and the island to come back here, a place she had run from months earlier, although you didn't know why, to try and make a new life for the both of you. Tattooing your name into the skin at her wrist just after you were born. *Mariposa.* And a little blue butterfly.

The pregnant woman pulls her coat to and walks over to talk to a member of staff standing near the barriers. You glance at your phone: two messages now. One from your mother: *Trains are being cancelled, I think. Where have you got to? x.* One from the girl: *Fucking snow. Ain't going out in this. So, come here or don't yeah?* The whirlpool fades and is replaced by a low flame. Then a branching of fire within you until you are blazing. Had your mother felt this same burning when she fled from your father? Is that what gave her the fuel to run? You type a message to the girl: *Not coming. Keep the books or get rid, yeah?* You head for the barriers and crunch over the grey snow towards the bus station. Through City Square and onto Boar Lane, along Call Lane and New York Street, arriving at the stop just as the number 36 pulls in and parks, its engine idling. You wait for the two people on it to get off, then climb on board, sitting on the bottom at the back, clutching your rucksack close to your belly. Hugging it tight.

Let me know you're OK.

You vibrate as the engine turns over, people climbing on and shivering as they pull gloves further up their wrists, scarves around their chins. You read your mother's messages again, begin to type, then send the text, sit back. Take a book out of your bag and begin to read, even though you thought you'd never read again, had only taken the book to bulk up your bag. After a page, the bus reverses out of its space, windscreen wipers pushing flakes from the glass, heat from the vents blowing warmth onto your boots and all around your ankles.

Your first text: *Coming back on the bus. Going to the Scandi café.* Your second: *Meet me if you want. Gonna get food.* You think of the waffles they serve there. Like oversized flowers on a wooden board, split into heart-shaped segments and with little dishes of cream and compote sitting in circular dips near the edge of the board. You think of the little hidey hole booth they have, with the opening at the front which lets you see the till and the tables near to it, the window with the café's name on, written in a thin white font the same colour as snow. The whole café will smell of cinnamon and gravlax, will be filled with steam and the hiss of the coffee machine, the clink of cups and cutlery. You will order for the both of you, then sit and sip your coffee as you wait for your mother to arrive. There will be the hum of voices that you'll tune into sometimes, tune out of mostly. Conversations about children and school. About work and bosses. About lovers – both lost and found. Your mother will arrive in her long coat with the robin brooch, a woollen hat pulled low over her brow. Spotting you through the glassless window of the booth, then sitting as the food is brought to your table. You won't speak to each other but will instead both just sit and pick up your knives, begin to spread first the cream and then the compote onto one of the segments before lifting a waffle heart to your mouths and taking a bite.

The snow will continue to fall in the streets, the heat of bodies and food turning the windows misty as you drink and eat. The outside world will become blurry as rainbows, the bodies of people turned to smears of colour through the hazy glass. 'Mum,' you'll say after you pick up your last piece, holding it close to your mouth but not looking at her. 'There's something I need to tell you.' She won't say anything then but will instead just look at you, watch as you take another bite, the waffle almost gone. Her small mouth – the same size as yours – will be open a little as she watches you. The final piece of waffle going into your mouth. The last bit of cream melting on your tongue until you can no longer taste it.

Little arrows

At night the robins come.

She knows because of the footprints in the snow along the window ledge, which aren't there when she goes to bed but are when she gets up in the morning. Black little arrows that trail from one side of the ledge to the other, then back again. Dirtying the white. Even when fresh snowfall comes and covers them up, the tracks are always back again by the morning. Not just at her bedroom window but on all the ledges – upstairs and down. Some of them facing the other way too as if the birds have turned away from the house or towards it. The little marks deeper there, darker, as if the robins stayed for a time. Still. Watching. The way they're positioned gives the woman the feeling of being singled out. Monitored. The arrows – the deep, the dark – appearing to point in at the windows or, maybe, if she thinks about it too much, point in at her.

It isn't just the tracks that make her think it's robins, but the sounds too. Those high-pitched trills and chirrups that are without any obvious repetition or phrasing. She has heard them sing many times before. Not just in winter. It's a misconception to think robins only appear around Christmas, and she has told people this; most recently the children at school a few weeks ago. 'Look for them in summer too,' she said. 'The ones with the red here.' And she touched her neck and just below her throat.

Later, to Carole, the teacher, she said, 'They're quite romantic really, aren't they?'

'Aggressive more like.'

'Oh? They make me think of hearts, with the red. Big, bold hearts.'

'Or blood,' said Carole, lines like quotation marks between her eyebrows.

The light was grey through the windows, she remembered. The forecast had mentioned something about snowfall; about the possibility of it arriving over the coming weeks.

Since the snows came, brightening the nights, the robins haven't just been singing in the day but in the dark too, when she's been trying but failing to sleep. Long, fast sections of song which rise and fall in pitch. Each note needle-thin. Followed by slower verses of squeaks and squeals. And every now and again, especially when she's on the verge of dreams, harsher, more urgent sounds. An alarm call of sorts. A sound that warns of predators, of approaching danger, perhaps. Of something being wrong. *Tseee*, is the sound the robins make in the night-time. *Tseee. Tseee. Tseee.*

She had only been in the village a month when the job came up. A classroom assistant at Little Acorns – the pre-school attached to the primary just over the bridge. She had got chatting to the school secretary at the village coffee shop one day, as they both queued for chai lattes and cranberry muffins. The secretary, Helen, had told her about the post. 'The pay isn't much,' she said. 'But the kids are great. And if you've got a qualification and experience, then you're probably in with a good chance.' Helen leaned in closer then. 'In all honesty,' she said. 'They're desperate. The previous girl didn't even work her notice out so they need someone quick.'

The phone call for an interview came a couple of days later. Helen told her that, because of the money, it was only between her and someone else – a young woman barely out of college and with no previous employments. And with her being nearby, as well as having what they needed, she was almost a shoe-in for it. It was only a couple of hours after the interview that she was offered the post. 'Do I need to know anything beforehand?' she asked. 'Do anything?'

'No,' the headteacher said to her on the phone. 'Just come in once your DBS check is back. All will become clear. We look forward to working with you, Laura.'

ᛦᛦᛦᛘᛘᛘ

It was the second week in November when she started – around the time the staff in Little Acorns started to think about what Christmas activities they could do with the children in December.

Some of them spoke about drawing Christmas cards for Mummy and Daddy, about making tree decorations using the lids of margarine tubs and covering them with coloured paper and glitter, threading them with string. The 'footprint robins' were her idea. There would be trays of brown paint on the floor that the children could press their bare feet into. Then they would place them onto paper, the heel making the robin's head, the ball the bulk of its body, their toes becoming feathers that would stick out at the back. All they would need to do then was use red paint for the beak and the breast, orange for the legs – and a dot of black to give the bird a small and beady eye in the middle of its head.

She remembered making such a robin herself as a little girl – the cool of the paint on the sole of her foot, then pushing down until the brown transferred itself onto the paper. She was helped to draw the beak and the legs, the bright red of the breast. But what she remembered most was the light inside her at how it looked when she'd finished, how like a robin. She couldn't wait to carry it out at home time, show it her mother at the gate; her mother who always said robins reminded her of Laura's father because of the one he'd whittled for her as a love token, out of a small piece of found wood. Her heart thumped at the thought of her mother's eyes brightening as she looked at the painted robin, the same way they brightened whenever she talked about Laura's dad – the man who had left them after she was born. She imagined her mother being so moved that she lifted Laura up, holding her tight, in the way she never did. The winter sun was low and bright as she placed her painting down on the table to dry. It was so strong it lit up the ripples in the paper, the ripples that were there because the sheets had warped from being wet. She was hardly able to stop herself from running out with it straight away.

Something happened after that which she still cannot explain – something to do with a new girl standing and looking at the paintings, her hand reaching out and its fingers dragging down Laura's painting until the brown bled into the red, the orange legs bending and breaking, the robin's round eye becoming a thin black stripe that slid out of the bird's head and into the white around it. There was a heat inside her at this, a grabbing and scratching that left her with spit on her chin and red beneath her fingernails. She remembered the new girl becoming a blur to her, then a strange bird-like screeching, the sight of gouges clawed out of skin. Then there were arms around her, so tight she could not breathe or move. Arms that squeezed and pulled her out of the classroom and into another room which she was placed inside of, locked into. A space referred to as the sick room.

In a while her mother came. Called by the teacher even though it was hours before she was due. She could see but not hear the teacher talking to her through the square pane of glass. The two of them looking in at her, then away again. Her mother's face blank. When the door opened, her mother did not come in, did not speak. Instead, Laura went towards her, reached for her hand. But her mother did not seem to see it and so did not take it.

She doesn't remember much else, except walking home, her mother silent beside her. And then, as they got back, moving into their dark hallway, Laura closing the door. Her mother stopped but didn't turn. She watched her take the little wooden robin out of her handbag then turn it over before putting it back. 'I'm not sure whose child you are,' she said, finally, her voice low in the dusky light. 'But you couldn't have come from us, behaving like that. Maybe he'd still be here if…' but she didn't finish whatever it was she had wanted to say.

She tries to cover her ears at night when the robins come. She will lie in bed, hear them singing in the blackness, those thin, clawed feet scarring the snow. She uses her fists to try and keep the noises out but she can't get the position right; there is always some sound that gets in. It's as if the song can travel through blood and bone. Burrowing in. Sometimes she's thought she's seen their shadows through the yellow velvet curtains, moving backward and forward on the ledge. But she is sure she's imagining that. For a start, there isn't any light out there that could make such silhouettes of them. Turning them into shadows. She breathes deep. Tries not to see the shapes of their footprints behind her eyes – those thin dark lines, the pointing arrows. She wishes she could reach into her skull to pull the shapes out, crumble them to nothing, stop them stamping around inside her, but all she can think is:

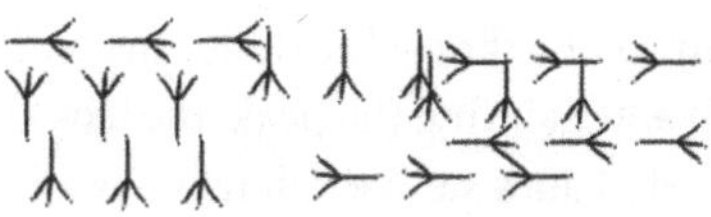

She helped the children take off socks and shoes, roll up trousers, some of them squealing as they got ready to press their feet into the trays of paint on the classroom floor. Most of them listened to her, about not being silly, about pushing their feet down onto the paper without moving them, then putting them straight into the other trays with the clean water and towels beside them. Not spreading the paint all over the floor.

Sometimes she had to try to hold the children's feet in place, to stop them wiggling them. Most behaved, did as they were told, then marvelled at the brown shape that did not yet look like a robin but would before long.

Melodie was a big girl for three, with thick arms and legs, teeth that she would grit when concentrating on malleable play or in the sand pit. She was the last of the children to have a go and the one, according to Carole, who was most promising when it came to painting. The child pulled off her shoes and socks and did as Laura asked, keeping her foot still as she pressed down hard. Laura held onto the paper as the girl lifted her foot, her heart stuttering because of how the brown had transferred, so there were hardly any missing bits of paint on the robin's body at all, no splashes marring the white.

‘Well done, Melodie – that’s great,’ Laura said. To which the child gritted then ungritted her teeth, her cheeks flushing for a moment. ‘Shall we…?’ And she helped the girl clean and wipe her foot, put her socks and shoes back on, before sitting down with her at the table, ready to help her paint the rest of the bird.

Melodie’s jaw was tight as she bent over, first swiping the bright red paint along the body to make the breast, then cleaning the brush and painting the beak, the legs and, finally, the black of the eye. Laura sat back, having hardly helped at all. ‘Wow,’ she said. ‘That’s brilliant.’ And she remembered, again, her own robin from years ago – how like this one it was, how well the child had done with it. Something inside her burst and broke then, making her eyes wetter than before.

Laura stood up then, sneaked her phone out of her pocket, pressed the button for the camera and leaned forward, making sure the edges of the screen aligned with the edges of the sheet so that nothing of the child or the table could be seen. ‘I’m just going to…’ she said, waiting for the camera to focus so she could take a photo. She felt a fluttering inside her at the thought of sending the picture to her mother, then writing the words that would accompany it: ‘This looks exactly like the one I made years ago. I wish you’d seen it. I’m sure you’d have loved it.’

Just as the camera focused though and Laura was about to press the button, Melodie’s hand appeared in the shot; four little fingers and a thumb which hovered over the bird before slapping down – then circling and circling until the robin’s head and body, its beak and legs became a swirling mush of brown with streaks of orange and red fireworking through it. The bird no longer visible at all. Laura remembers the heat and a reaching out, grabbing the child’s arm. But the rest is a haze that sometimes returns at night in snatches of colour, rushes of sound: a pressing in of nails, the appearance of a dull red that is not as bright as the robin's breast, the scree-screeching of someone who is not her. And then. And then. A dragging away from the bright of the classroom and out into the street, beneath clouds which look heavy with snow. A single flake tumbling and falling out of the sky, before landing and perching on the edge of an eyelash.

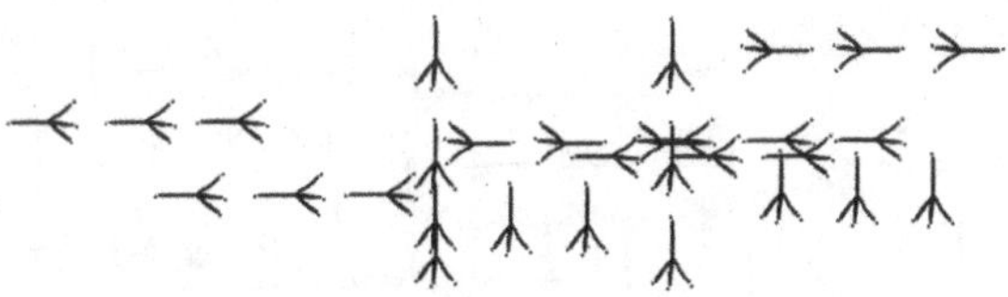

The snow fell fast that night – after she had been interviewed at the station, her words written on a form that she had to read and then sign. The white brought the robins with it. Walking up and down the ledges outside her windows, turning one way then another; leaving their little arrows everywhere. Pointing, pointing, pointing. Aiming in at her. She can see the footprints even more as the weeks pass; in the daytime, the night-time, when her eyes are open or even when they're closed. She cannot seem to get rid of them. She has tried to phone her mother many times, texted twice as much – but, still, she hasn't been able to reach her. Her calls unanswered; her messages unread.

She is lying in bed again now in the dark. There is that *tseee* sound again as she tries to sleep. *Tseee. Tseee. Tseee.* The little shadows are at the window too. Moving faster now, growing bigger as if there are more of the birds there. Herding in a way robins never would. Assembling. For what she doesn't know. She closes her eyes, rubs at her forehead to try and clear her mind, but all she can see are those footprints. Laying tracks across her brain. *Tseee. Tseee. Tseee.* And now there is a scratching; the scritching of little feet against glass. A sharding of sound that splinters and cracks. The flapping of wings. The robins swoop then, fly at her in the bed. Stomping. Stamping. Their small beaks opening and widening in the dark, biting down until her own blood comes.

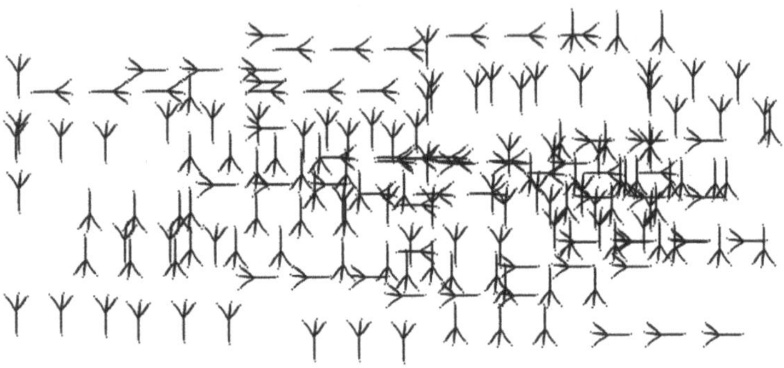

The monolith

It appears overnight. The monolith. A tall black column like an oversized tombstone in the yard.

At sunrise Maggie looks out, blinks at a burst of light firing off one corner. 'What's that?' she says, and blinks again. 'God.' She rubs at the window with the side of a fist, as if doing that will somehow make it go away.

She reaches for the phone and presses the memory button and the number one.

After seven rings Carl answers. 'Hello,' he says, his voice cracking from sleep.

'There's a monolith in the yard,' she says, a hiss like rain on the line. She says it again, only louder. 'There's a monolith in the yard.'

'What?' he says. 'What are you talking about?'

She squints out again and thinks she sees a ripple across the monolith, as if it's made of black liquid. 'I'm not joking, Carl. There's a monolith in the yard.'

'I heard you the first two times,' he says, sounding as if he's trying to suppress a yawn. 'A monolith? Like from 2001? That kind of monolith?'

She rolls her eyes. 'What other kind of monolith is there?'

Carl doesn't speak but in the background Maggie can just make out the low mumble of a woman's voice. She imagines him with someone else – the two of them curled up in bed like a pair of cats: her stretching and stroking him with slender, reaching arms; his legs entwined in hers.

'Carl?' she says, kicking her foot against the skirting board. 'Say something.'

She hears Carl put his fingers over the mouthpiece. It makes a scuffling noise that irritates her ear. She pulls the phone away for a few seconds before putting it back but she can't hear anything. Another scuffle and he removes his hand.

'Maggie,' he says. 'I don't know what you're expecting from me.'

Her foot kicks harder.

The woman with Carl talks louder now, her voice echoey as if she's speaking from his en-suite bathroom. 'What's she playing at?' the woman says.

Maggie thinks of this woman washing in Carl's sink or using his toothbrush and stops kicking. 'Can you tell whoever that is that I'm not playing at anything? I just thought you might want to know what's happening here.'

'Tamsin,' he says. 'Her name is Tamsin.'

'Then would you mind telling her that I'm not playing at anything?'

'OK,' he says and moves the phone away from his mouth. 'She said she's not playing at anything.'

She hears the woman say, 'Of course not.'

'Excuse me,' says Maggie. 'But she doesn't even know me.'

'True,' he says. 'Be quiet, Tamsin.'

Maggie sees next door's cat on the yard wall – a clump of grey fur with a fluffy tail that looks shocked with static. It sniffs the air and turns to look at the monolith, leans a leg down, as if dipping a toe into water, then jumps into Maggie's yard. It sniffs again then slowly pads towards the tall, black pillar, stopping every now and then as if trying not to trip an alarm system.

Maggie bangs on the window. 'Hey,' she says to the cat but it doesn't respond.

'What are you hey-ing at?' says Carl.

She bangs louder and the cat turns before carrying on walking.

'Maggie?' says Carl.

'Cefor,' she says. 'It's in my yard.'

The cat reaches the monolith and puts its head down, sniffing at the base. Its tail swishes over the paving slabs – the tip flicking up and down like someone tapping a foot.

'Cefor,' he says, a playfulness in his voice. 'The imaginary cat.'

'Shoo.' Maggie bangs on the window again. 'Shoo.' Then she smiles too. 'It isn't imaginary. It's lived there for years.'

'Well, I never saw it.'

Maggie leans so close to the window that it begins to steam up from her breath. She wipes the mist with her sleeve and steps back. 'Well, you were oblivious to a lot of things.'

'Thanks,' he says, pretending to be wounded.

The cat stops sniffing and instead just sits at the side of the monolith looking up at it. It blinks slowly – the kind of action that, in the cat world, is supposed to mean contentment.

'So anyway,' he says, 'this monolith...'

'That's what I said.'

'Are you sure there's one there?' he says.

Maggie stands tall and thrusts her shoulders back. 'Do you think I'm making things up or something?'

'No,' says Carl. 'It just sounds a bit strange, that's all.'

She hears Tamsin say something that she can't make out.

'Look,' he says, 'I've got to go, OK?'

Just then she thinks she sees the black ripple make waves across the monolith's surface again and she leans forward. But as she does this the cat lifts a paw up and touches it, in the same way it might reach for a dangling piece of wool. As soon as it does this there is a sudden rush of movement and the cat is dragged inside. There's just a smudge of grey in Maggie's vision at the exact spot where the cat was. She gasps.

'What is it?' says Carl. 'What's up?'

'Oh,' she says. 'Oh.' It feels as if invisible hands are squeezing her vocal chords tight shut.

'What's going on?' says Tamsin.

'Maggie?' says Carl.

But Maggie can't speak.

'I'm coming over,' he says. 'I want to see what's going on.'

Maggie drops the phone into its cradle. There are tears forming in her eyes that she tries to blink and then rub away. She fumbles in the drawer for the key to the back door then rushes out into the yard. She searches around without going too near the monolith but the cat has gone. 'Cefor,' she calls out. 'Cefor.' But the only thing remaining is the bell that dangled from the front of its collar like a small, silver planet.

She stands at the back door, staring back and forth between the bell and the monolith, as a chilly breeze lifts the hairs on her arms and makes goosebumps stand like a rash of tiny hills all over her body. The surface of the monolith is now as still and frozen as a black, winter river. Nothing moving, no hint of life.

*

Thirty minutes later Carl arrives with Tamsin. Maggie watches his four by four swerve into the steep drive and brake hard near the steps. He climbs out and strides to the door while Tamsin checks her hair in the mirror on the back of the visor before following him. Maggie, clutching a mug of tea, opens the door to them. Tamsin, a tall, horse-limbed woman, lets her eyes linger over Maggie's stomach before lifting them to look her in the face.

'What's going on?' says Carl, his brow furrowed as he glances over Maggie. Then he steps past her and into the house. Tamsin hovers at the door, a huge designer bag hanging from her arm – its eyelets gaping.

'Come in,' says Maggie, catching the faint smell of Chanel No. 19 as Tamsin passes – the same perfume Carl had once regularly bought for her.

Maggie follows them both indoors. They look out at the yard. She sips her tea, feeling its heat on her tongue before swallowing it.

'It's a monolith,' says Carl.

'Well spotted,' says Maggie. 'But I did say it was.'

Tamsin raises her eyes to Carl but he doesn't notice.

'So what were all the hysterics about?' he asks.

'What hysterics?' says Maggie, going into the kitchen and switching on the kettle, its blue light flickering over the counter like watery sapphires. She senses a shift in the atmosphere and turns to find Carl in the doorway.

'On the phone,' he says.

The kettle fills the air with a hushing sound as Maggie pulls two cups from the cupboard. 'It wasn't hysterics,' she says. 'The cat went inside that thing. It frightened me.'

Carl strokes his chin. 'The monolith?'

'Yes.'

'Really?'

Maggie feels a flare shoot up inside her and her voice grows louder. 'It – went – in – the – monolith. I'm not making it up.' She throws teabags into the cups. 'If you don't believe me you might as well go now.'

Carl folds his arms and leans into the door frame. 'It just seems crazy.'

She pours water into the cups and stirs so fast with the spoon that tea spills onto the worktop. 'Well, crazy or not, the cat's gone.' She squeezes the teabags and drops them into the bin. 'I didn't know who else to ring.'

He steps forward and touches her on the shoulder. 'It's OK,' he says. Tamsin appears in the doorway, her gaze lingering on Maggie's shoulder. 'Give me the key, Mags. I want to go outside and have a look for myself.'

Carl rattles the key in the lock and goes out into the yard. Maggie's temples pulse like silent drums.

*

Carl covers every inch of the yard. After that he goes out through the back gate, calling for the cat all the while.

'There's just the bell,' shouts Maggie. 'That's all that's left.'

Tamsin hoists her bag further up her arm. Her gold bracelets clink. 'You can buy bells.'

Maggie turns to her, dumbfounded. 'Why would I buy a bell?'

'For this whole fantasy,' she says. 'To make it more realistic.'

'Fantasy?' says Maggie. Tamsin nods.

'And I suppose I bought that too,' says Maggie, pointing to the monolith.

Tamsin shrugs and raises an eyebrow. 'It's only a big headstone. They're not that hard to come by.'

'So I dragged one home from the cemetery and scraped the words off?' Maggie shakes her head. 'And what's happened to the cat?'

Tamsin pauses and looks at Maggie's stomach again. 'Maybe there wasn't a cat in the first place. Who knows?'

Maggie's hands automatically go to her belly, covering it like a shell made of fingers. 'Carl knows there was a cat. Don't be ridiculous.'

'Well, he doesn't really, does he?' says Tamsin, one nostril and the side of her mouth lifting as if smelling something unpleasant. 'He never saw it. He hasn't got any evidence.'

'Just because he didn't see it didn't mean it didn't exist,' says Maggie.

'Very Zen and very deep,' says Tamsin, tossing her hair over her shoulder. 'Especially if we're still talking about a cat.'

Maggie feels a lump like a rock in her throat, so hard that she has to force herself to breathe.

Tamsin pushes her chest out. 'Anyway, maybe we'll have our own one day. A real one that is.'

Maggie notices the lilac semi-circles and heavy lines that lie beneath Tamsin's eyes as if she's lain awake for days on end. She swallows hard. 'Why have you got a problem with me?' she asks gently. 'What have I done to you?'

The lightness of Maggie's voice seems to loosen something in Tamsin too and she lifts a hand to her mouth and nibbles her nails, already nipped down to below the tips of her fingers. These two things – the eyes, the nails – make Maggie think of silent alarms, unconsciously triggered.

'You can't have him back,' Tamsin says, so quiet Maggie can hardly hear her.

'What?' says Maggie.

'You can't have him back.'

Just then Carl calls out from somewhere beyond the yard wall and he appears at the gate holding a bundle of grey fur.

The cat is bouncing its nose to his chin in a display of feline affection.

'Cefor,' says Maggie, her mouth fallen open.

'Is this him?' says Carl, tugging lightly on the cat's ear. 'He was sitting on a wall a few doors up. He looks fine, perfectly fine.'

The cat's eyes are a violet-blue and remind her of the pansies that Carl placed in pots in the yard during their first year of marriage. She gulps at the suddenness of this memory – of Carl bending and moving them to find the best spot; the look of bright joy in his face as he turned to find her watching him do it.

Suddenly the cat leans its head forward. She touches it and the cat responds by pushing its soft face into her hand.

'See?' says Carl. 'He's fine.'

'He seems different,' says Maggie. 'Like a different cat. More peaceful somehow.'

'Cefor,' says Carl, rubbing his head roughly. 'Well, it's nice to meet you finally.' Maggie waits for the cat to growl or grumble but it doesn't: it just closes its eyes and lets itself be ravaged by Carl's big hands.

After a while Carl sits Cefor on the yard wall, picks the bell up from the floor and fixes it back onto the cat's collar.

Tamsin sighs loudly. 'Can we go now?'

'Hold on,' says Carl, as he watches Cefor tiptoe along the wall, turn back to them and then jump down into next door's yard.

Maggie turns to Tamsin, who is now folding her arms and staring at Carl. Her bag looks sunken like a dead weight. 'I didn't imagine it,' Maggie says to her.

Tamsin watches Carl. 'Carl?'

'Well,' says Carl. 'It's back now, that's the main thing.'

'I didn't,' says Maggie, this time to Carl. She notices how, for a few seconds, he stares at her and then Tamsin, a sad tugging at the edge of his mouth. His gaze drops to the ground and he shrugs.

Tamsin turns to go in the house. Maggie follows. But just as she's about to step indoors she turns and Carl is standing next to the monolith. Maggie sees its surface ripple and Carl, oblivious, lifting his hand towards it.

'No!' shouts Maggie.

Tamsin pushes Maggie out of the way and they both watch as Carl is dragged into the monolith without a sound. They gasp.

'Oh my God,' shouts Tamsin. 'Where's he gone?'

Maggie holds a hand to her chest. She can feel her heart pounding throughout her body. For a while she can hear nothing, as if her ears have been filled with water. When it returns Tamsin is still shouting at her.

*

Inside, Maggie makes tea with shaking hands. She offers a cup to Tamsin, who is standing at the window staring out into the yard, her eyes balls of pink jelly rimmed with smudges of black like coal dust. But when Tamsin refuses to take it from her she puts it on the windowsill instead.

'He'll be back,' says Maggie, breathing deep to soften the whirlwinds in her stomach. 'Cefor came back.'

Tamsin sniffs then dabs at her nose with a tissue. 'Cefor,' she says and tuts. Then she takes the cup and gulps from it, seemingly unaware of its heat. She turns to Maggie. 'This was your plan all along, wasn't it? Get him here, trap him.'

Maggie turns to look at the monolith and sees a streak of white down its front from a passing bird. 'You're giving me too much credit,' she says, her voice low.

'Well, he's not yours,' says Tamsin, her chin trembling like water.

Maggie sips at the tea without tasting it then puts her cup down. 'He's not anybody's,' she says. 'Least of all mine.'

A gust of wind makes the window frame crack like a bone. Suddenly Tamsin's eyes crease up and she forces the tissue into their corners to try and stem the tears. Maggie touches her on the arm, ready to retract her hand should Tamsin flinch.

'I was like you, always worried about losing him,' says Maggie, taking a shuddering breath in. 'And then I lost him and – ' she stops.

Tamsin is still for a time before nodding slowly, the tissue still pushed into her eyes. Maggie rubs Tamsin's arm.

Just then she looks out again and the monolith appears darker, as if it's changed to a deeper shade of black. She squints at it to try and work out whether she is imagining it or not. As she watches it seems to pulse to an even darker colour and it appears to be smaller than just a few seconds earlier. Maggie runs for the door. As she fiddles with the handle Tamsin pushes up against her back, desperate to get out.

'What's going on?' says Tamsin, frantic.

'Something's happening.'

They stumble out into the yard. Cefor is sitting on the wall again, watching the monolith.

'What is it?' says Tamsin, a hand to her throat.

The monolith pulses stronger and continues to grow smaller as they watch.

'Oh, God,' says Maggie. 'It's shrinking.'

Tamsin screams and covers her mouth with her hands. 'I thought you said he'd be coming back?'

Maggie doesn't answer but instead steps nearer to the monolith. It is now half the size it was when it first appeared.

'Carl!' shouts Tamsin from behind her. 'Come out!'

Maggie leans forward to try and get a closer look but all she can see is the throbbing blackness. Then Tamsin is at her side, reaching out.

'For God's sake, Tamsin. Don't touch it.'

Tamsin pulls her hand back. The monolith shrinks further. Cefor jumps down into the yard and sits beside them. Maggie looks down at the cat and it meows at her without making a sound. She can see the ribbed roof of its mouth like a small, pink cave.

'We have to get him out,' says Tamsin, sobbing.

'How?' shouts Maggie, the monolith now the size of an upright shoebox. 'We can't.'

The three of them continue to watch as the monolith becomes as small as a pebble on the stone flags.

'It's going to vanish,' says Tamsin, her hands cradling her face. 'It's nearly gone.'

The monolith, now a black dot, winks in and out of existence for a few seconds before finally blinking out for good. Maggie, Tamsin and the cat stare at the ground. Then Cefor steps forward, leans its head down and licks at the place where the monolith was, leaving a patch of damp on the flag like a brushstroke. The cat meows silently again and she can see grey dust peppering its tongue.

'Oh, God,' says Tamsin, hugging herself. 'He's gone.'

Maggie crouches down, putting the tips of her fingers against the flags to steady herself. She feels small and frail.

Cefor crawls up into her lap. She lets the cat nestle into the space between her legs, its violet-blue eyes staring up at her until she feels as if she's swaying.

Tamsin falls to her knees, pale as a candle. Cefor's tail twitches against her leg.

As Maggie looks into the cat's eyes, she has the sensation of falling into them – swirling around and down until she is no longer sure who or where she is. And then she hears Carl's voice, floating inside her head like smoke, wandering among her atoms and molecules in a sparkling dance of mist.

'I could have come back,' he says, his voice light and free. He's like a mound of shining cloud. 'But I decided not to – at least for a while.' He sounds as if he's smiling. 'I hope you both –' he fades out but then there's a humming sound and his voice returns. 'You're going to be fine,' he says.

Suddenly Carl's voice is gone and Maggie blinks, aware once more of her surroundings. She turns to Tamsin who, after a few seconds, awakens too.

The cat crawls out from Maggie's legs, runs to the wall and jumps over in one; his tail disappearing out of sight. Maggie feels the coldness of the stone then, chilling her skin.

'I heard him,' says Tamsin, looking about her.

'So did I,' says Maggie.

'He's not coming back.'

Without saying anything more Maggie rises from the floor and helps to pull Tamsin up. She hears the metallic ping of the cat's bell as he runs away from them. She stops to listen without speaking, Tamsin too, until the bell can no longer be heard. She becomes aware then of the silent vacuum that surrounds the two of them. And how, after a while, other sounds rush in to fill it.

Afterword: 'No time to mourn'[1]: Female characters and their preapocalyptic activities in the postapocalyptic short story

(This afterword was presented at the ENSFR Annual Conference on Short Fiction: Landscape and Temporality in Manchester, October 2023. It was later published in the journal Short Fiction in Theory and Practice *as a discussion of Carmen Maria Machado's short story 'Inventory', which helped to inspire the opening story in this collection.)*

Introduction

In *Flowers of Time: On Postapocalyptic Fiction*, Mark Payne says, apocalyptic fictions 'focus on the end of days itself' (Payne, 2020: 1) with the apocalyptic event being 'what comes to human beings from the outside, projecting them outside their accustomed forms of life in ways they could not have anticipated' (Payne, 2020: 9). In *After the End: Representations of the Post-Apocalypse*, James Berger argues that 'something remains *after the end*', though, such that 'The end is never the end' (Berger, 1999: 5), with the 'something' he speaks of being 'the *post-apocalypse*', which is, he asserts, 'usually the true object of the apocalyptic writer's concern' (Berger, 1999: 6).

This paper navigates ideas relating to notions of the end, in particular with regard to how female characters in postapocalyptic settings resist this often by continuing with

[1] From 'Inventory' (Machado, 2019: 43).

preapocalyptic activities, such as list-making or sculpture, in a bid to help them navigate what is a ruined or deeply changed world. I will consider such ideas by discussing Carmen Maria Machado's short story 'Inventory' (Machado, 2019) in the first part of the paper, and then presenting my own postapocalyptic short story 'Maybe the birds'; the story is in conversation with and acts as a creative response to 'Inventory'. During the discussion, I will engage primarily with Marco Caracciolo's article on 'Negative strategies and world disruption in postapocalyptic fiction' (Caracciolo, 2018), considering his ideas on 'the disrupted temporality of catastrophe', and his suggestion that there is a rupturing between the preapocalyptic and postapocalyptic worlds, which, he argues, leads to an absence with regard to depictions of the pre-world and is achieved through the use of 'negative strategies' in the language (Caracciolo, 2018: 222). In a questioning of this, I will argue how females in the short story, specifically Machado's and my own, can be seen to resist this apocalyptic rupture, and thereby resist the end, by continuing with preapocalyptic activities in the post-world. I will show how this ensures the presence, rather than absence, of the pre-world with the artefacts of such activities – lists and sculptures – becoming 'repositories of information' (Belknap, 2000: 41), which provide hope and act as carriers of the flame of human language and experience into post-world settings.

It is important to say that these preapocalyptic activities are carried out by females but can also be said to be gendered themselves, as in they are activities generally associated with women. For example, the artist Alice Instone, following research for her exhibition The Pram in the Hall (Instone, 2024), featuring women's to-do lists, 'found that women make a lot more lists than men' (*Woman's Hour*, 2023) and that this is possibly related to 'multi-tasking' and the 'complete wide spectrum of tasks' that women are expected to do, such as looking after children, parents and pets as well as working, doing housework, and so on. Academic Joanna Nolan, author of the book *Listful*, says that, 'perhaps, both men and women make lists but women make them with more enthusiasm… women are interested in the actual making of the list' and that this is possibly so 'we don't miss any of the unbelievable tasks we feel we have to achieve but also because we want a record that we can refer back to' (*Woman's Hour*, 2023). With regard to pottery and ceramics, Courtney Lee Weida argues that women are strongly associated with pottery and have been regarded as 'the first makers of clay objects' as well as 'often [being] associated with nature, earth, and domesticity or the home (features commonly linked with clay as a material)' (Weida, 2011: 1). However, she says, there is evidence of women's exclusion from the field including receiving 'profit and credit for their own ceramic work, and acknowledgement as leaders of the field of studio ceramics' (Weida, 2011: 1–2), although, she argues that '[h]istorical conceptions persist, including perceptions of ceramics as an "exclusively female activity" or "'naturalized' activity linked to females' (Weida, 2011: 2). This idea of gendered activities in the postapocalypse is not the subject of this paper though, but would prove to be an interesting area of investigation for future research.

I am focusing on female characters specifically in this article as it can be argued women are underrepresented in both the creative and critical literature with regard to the postapocalypse, with female resistance to the apocalyptic rupture, in particular, underexplored in fictional and critical contexts. Claire P. Curtis argues, for instance, that, 'There is a familiar trajectory to postapocalyptic fiction… [whereby] [t]raditionally, the main character [is]… typically a white male' (Curtis, 2010: 7–8), with females often portrayed as weaker and only taking on a supporting role: 'In the initial movements towards survival,' she says, '– finding food, finding or making shelter, the survivor stumbles upon a companion – usually someone *weaker* (a child, or a *young woman*)' (Curtis, 2010: 8; my emphasis). The short story, however, provides an opportunity to explore and challenge these ideas, as it provides a space for females to be at the heart of their own postapocalyptic narratives, placing them in positions of strength as opposed to weakness, and centring them in post-world settings and scenarios.

'Inventory'

'Inventory' by Carmen Maria Machado, from her acclaimed debut collection *Her Body & Other Parties* (Machado, 2019), is the story of an unnamed woman's experiences of the postapocalypse, told in a list format which also explores her sexual relationships from young adulthood to the age of thirty, when the story ends. The piece exemplifies what Marco Caracciolo terms a 'double vision' in postapocalyptic fiction, whereby we are 'mentally entertaining two worlds at the same time' – the pre- and post-worlds, the present and the absent – which, he says, 'serves as a poignant reminder of the material things and social structures that were lost in the catastrophic transition' (Caracciolo, 2018: 226), and implying, as Briohny Doyle argues, that the postapocalyptic world is 'haunted by memories of the pre-catastrophe world' (Doyle, 2015). To demonstrate this, Caracciolo uses Fibonacci's Kanizsa triangle (see

Figure 1) as a way to show the multiple realities that exist in postapocalyptic fiction – as shown by the 'present' triangle co-existing in the same space as the 'absent' one. For Caracciolo, this means that 'when we process a negative statement, we entertain its affirmative counterpart before fully parsing its negative meaning' (Caracciolo, 2018: 226), such that '[f]or a moment, a statement and its opposite appear to coexist' (Caracciolo, 2018: 226).

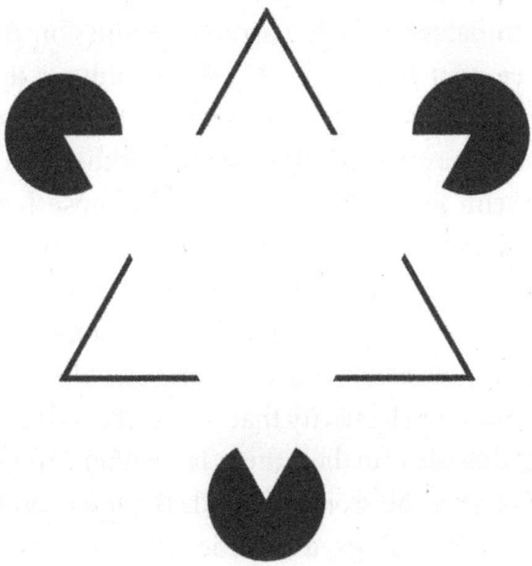

FIGURE 1: *The Kanizsa triangle*. (Fibonacci, CC BY-SA 3.0 <http://creativecommons.org/licenses/by-sa/3.0/>, via Wikimedia Commons.)

In 'Inventory', the two worlds we are entertaining include the woman's listing of various sexual experiences with both men and women, and also the gradual revealing of apocalyptic and postapocalyptic scenarios when outlining these encounters. There are references to both pre- and post-worlds throughout the story, meaning there is indeed a 'double vision' at play here. In the opening paragraph, for instance, we can see evidence of what Caracciolo terms 'negation' (Carraciolo, 2018: 226), where there is a 'strong sense of the disrupted temporality of catastrophe' caused by '"negative strategies" [which are] formal devices that leverage the underlying psychological structure of negation in order to confront readers with the absence of the preapocalyptic world' (Carraciolo, 2018: 222). This can be seen in Machado with the unnamed female narrator's admission that, 'I still have never seen *Jurassic Park*', which conjures up both an image of the film *Jurassic Park* as well as its absence, implied by her use of 'never seen'. This idea is solidified further in the next line with her realization that, 'I suppose I never will, now' (Machado, 2019: 33), which is the first hint given to the reader of the changed world the woman is situated in – the postapocalyptic world – where it is now no longer possible to watch a film such as *Jurassic Park,* presumably because there is no television or electricity that would allow this to happen.

Taking this idea further, there is another kind of double vision at play in the story too, with the focus on the woman's sexual relationships, as mentioned, alongside, as hinted here, the gradual revealing of the apocalyptic event, which has been caused by an unspecified virus. We can see this in the third paragraph, headed 'Two boys, one girl', where the narrator explains a sexual encounter with her then boyfriend – 'he encouraged me to make out with his friend's girlfriend. We kissed tentatively, then stopped' (Machado, 2019: 34) – but which ends with the memory of her boyfriend's mother finding her underwear and returning it 'laundered, without a word. It's weird to me how much I miss that floral, chemical smell of clean clothes. Now, all I can think about is fabric softener' (Machado, 2019: 34).

The paragraph gradually creates the sensation of double vision through the use of the image of clean, freshly washed clothes from the pre-world, which is summoned but then erased by the woman, as she speaks to us from her post-world, postapocalyptic point of view. This is done through her use of the word 'miss' which implies absence, and from the suggestion that she keeps thinking about fabric softener – something she would not do if this product was still present and available to her. This insight into the woman's thoughts and state of mind, implied through the use of negation, that is, the conjuring and then removing of the olfactory imagery of the 'floral, chemical smell of clean clothes', suggests that clothes in the post-world are now unclean and dirty because such items as detergent and fabric softener no longer exist in such a changed world.

Machado achieves this 'double vision' specifically through her use of lists, with the protagonist's listing of sexual relationships acting as a structuring device for the story. The story is split into separate paragraphs, each of which describes a particular encounter, such as in the first paragraph, which opens with the words, 'One girl', and goes on to explore the narrator's developing sexuality with another girl – 'I pulled up my shirt, she pulled up hers, and we just stared at each other' (Machado, 2019: 33) – with the listing format continuing until the reference to 'One woman' (Machado, 2019: 42) at the story's close. This section details the narrator's final relationship with another woman, who, we discover, is infected and who the narrator abandons in order to go and live on her own on a nearby island. After all, in such a postapocalyptic scenario, 'There was no time to mourn' (Machado, 2019: 43).

This idea of 'double vision' is present with the lists not only used as a structuring device – and the title 'Inventory' referring to this idea also – but by forming part of the narrator's characterization through her own use of lists in the story, which I will explore later.

In a questioning of Caracciolo, though, I want to argue that not all elements of the pre-world are conjured and negated in postapocalyptic fiction, certainly with regard to the short story, as can be seen in 'Inventory'. Caracciolo's argument that, usually, 'postapocalyptic fiction is set in the post-world and only *implies* the pre-world as a backdrop to the plot' (Caracciolo, 2018: 224; author's emphasis) can, I feel, be questioned here. Instead, through the use of list-making, which plays 'an important role in our everyday lives' (Alber, 2016: 342) whether this be 'to-do lists, checklists… shopping lists… playlists or hit lists' (Alber, 2016: 342), the pre-world is fully present, and not just a backdrop to the plot. Indeed, it is central to and at the forefront of this postapocalyptic story, as affirmed by Machado having her narrator use lists but also by her adopting this as a structuring device for the piece. For the unnamed central character, list-making is a way for her to achieve some level of order or reliability in what has become a deeply troubled world, using them both for comfort as well as survival, summoning and leaning into them as she navigates her way from pre-world through apocalyptic and postapocalyptic settings.

Here, the woman often makes lists in order to deal with uncomfortable situations and feelings both before the epidemic has taken hold as well as afterwards. For example, four pages into the story, when a sexual encounter with a man she's met at a bar ends with him getting angry and slamming the door on his way out, the narrator describes herself as being '[r]evved from adrenaline' (Machado, 2019: 36) and that, because of this, she then makes a list of animals she's owned – 'seven, including my two betta fish, who died within a week of each other' (Machado, 2019: 36) – followed by a list of the spices in pho: 'Cloves, cinnamon, star anise, coriander, ginger, cardamom pods' (Machado, 2019: 36). In a later section, as the virus progresses and the death toll rises, the narrator hears that 'the virus had somehow reached Nebraska' (Machado, 2019: 39) and, because this is near to her, she at that point decides to leave her home and go east. Again, she refers to making lists as a way to cope with the anxiety of the situation:

> *I left the garden, the plot where my dog was buried, the pine table where I'd anxiously made so many lists – trees that began with m: maple, mimosa, mahogany, mulberry, magnolia, mountain ash, mangrove, myrtle, states that I had lived in: Iowa, Indiana, Pennsylvania, Virginia, New York – leaving unreadable jumbles of letters imprinted in the soft wood. (Machado, 2019: 39)*

Here, list-making relating to trees or states she's lived in are a way for her to manage the anxiety of existing in a dramatically changing or changed world. Indeed, using them helps to ground her and keep her planted and rooted in the world; the ecological use of language no mistake here as the woman recalls the names of trees, for instance, almost like an incantation or affirmation to try and ensure she stays connected to and part of the world. The act of writing them into wood also, perhaps, helps to ensure the human names of things – trees, states – survive, even if humans do not. An affirmation of presence rather than absence.

In the concluding part of the story, lists play a vital role in the woman's bid for survival and her attempts to resist notions of the end. In the final section, for instance, we are told that a woman she has met has symptoms of the virus: 'Her skin the dark purple of compounded bruises, the whites of her eyes shot through with red, and blood leaking from the misty beds of her fingernails' (Machado, 2019: 43). But instead of the narrator staying there and perhaps comforting the woman – her final lover, if we are to believe the listing structure of the story – she checks her own face for symptoms, finding her own eyes still clear, and then tells us, 'There was no time to mourn. I consulted my emergency list and its supplies' (Machado, 2019: 43). She then gathers the items together and leaves the mainland for the nearby island, the only place it seems she can go to get away from the dangerous, infected bodies of others. The implication here is that the list – the emergency list – will help the woman to keep going, to survive, for now at least. And her use of them in the final lines of the story demonstrate how she will continue to use them to resist the end for as long as she is able to. 'I drank water,' she tells us, 'and set up my tent and began to make lists. Every teacher beginning with preschool. Every job I've ever had. Every home I've ever lived. Every person I've ever had. Every person who has probably loved me' (Machado, 2019: 43) – the final two lines possibly providing the starting point for this particular story, with her listing of former loves and lovers throughout it. A device that creates a kind of circularity as well as resonance.

The narrowing of the woman's options though, her retreat to an island with presumably limited supplies, her observation in the final two lines of the story that, 'I keep thinking I can see the virus blooming on the horizon like a sunrise. I realize the world will continue to turn, even with no people on it. Maybe it will go a little faster' (Machado, 2019: 43) are bleak and poignant. All of this implying that *her* end may be near, if not *the* end (remember Berger's assertion that 'The end is never the end' (Berger, 1999: 5), and that, 'There is always some remainder, some post-apocalyptic debris' (Berger, 1999: 34)).

Maybe, then, the pre-world activity of list-making, which leaks into the post-world as in 'Inventory', is one way to resist the end, to counteract Caracciolo's ideas about the 'disrupted temporality of catastrophe' (Caracciolo, 2018: 222). As Robert Belknap says, 'Lists have been used for varied purposes throughout history. Among other things, they serve to enumerate, account, remind, memorialize, order' (Belknap, 2000: 40). They reflect 'our compulsive need to impose order on chaos… they provide orientation' (Alber, 2016: 342–343). Lists, therefore, re-impose a chronology of sorts, helping to maintain a kind of pre-world temporality rather than a chaotic or disrupted post-world one, an attempt, perhaps, to keep the pre-world metronome ticking. As Margaret Atwood says, 'within each utopia, a concealed dystopia; within each dystopia, a hidden utopia' (Atwood, 2011: 85). In this story, perhaps, lists perform that function of utopian seed of hope as characters respond to and navigate dystopian apocalyptic and postapocalyptic settings.

In my own short story, 'Maybe the birds', it is not list-making but pottery that is the pre-apocalyptic activity which leaks through into the post-world; but both are activities which involve hand and mind and which are reminiscent somewhat of Ursula K. Le Guin's thoughts on 'handmind', interpreted as 'craft' by Mark Payne in *Flowers of Time* (Payne, 2020: 8). This is outlined in Le Guin's novel *Always Coming*

Home, a postapocalyptic story set in the distant future and which focuses on the lives and stories of the Kesh people. Here, she writes:

> *Nothing we do is better than the work of handmind. When mind uses itself without the hands it runs the circle and may go too fast; even speech using the voice only may go too fast. The hand that shapes the mind into clay or written word slows thought to the gait of things and lets it be subject to accident and time. (Le Guin, 2019: 210; my emphasis)*

To me this demonstrates what may be happening in both mine and Machado's stories: hand and mind working together through clay or written word to slow thought, calm the mind, bring order; Caracciolo's 'disrupted temporality' of the postapocalypse restored to the slow and regular tick of the pre-world metronome.

Payne's idea of 'craft' is present in both of our stories through the pre-world activities that lie at the heart of them. In Machado, the central character 'makes' lists, which, as Belknap says, are 'deliberate structures, built with care and *craft*' (Belknap, 2000: 54; my emphasis), while in my own story, the character 'makes' bird voice-boxes in clay, which is also a craft but one that relies on artistic ability instead. But there is more than just 'craft' going on here. The lists and voice-box sculptures perform a wider function. They are 'repositories of information' (Belknap, 2000: 41): one for the 'pleasurable infinitude of language' (Belknap, 2000: 35), the other for sound, in particular birdsong. As Belknap argues, 'Lists are adaptable containers that hold information selected from the mind-deep pool of possibility' (Belknap, 2000: 39), such that they are vessels that are 'meaningful to those who read or access them' (Belknap, 2000: 41). In my own story, the small sculptures play a similar role by being 'containers' of the kinds of sounds that birds can make. Both, though, are an attempt to ensure information survives in the postapocalypse, regardless of whether human beings themselves survive or not. They are a way to resist apocalyptic rupture, resist the end.

The similarities between mine and Machado's stories are clear: both are postapocalyptic, both have a central female narrator who is navigating a changed world as a result of an unspecified virus closing in on her, both check their eyes for signs of infection. But, mainly, our two characters are similar in their attempts to resist the end, in their hopes to affirm presence rather than absence, to – as my character says – 'Keep making. Keep on.' In 'Maybe the birds', my character is a potter, usually of plates and dishes, but who now that there are no more birds, decides to recreate bird syrinxes, or voice boxes, so that she can hang them in the trees to ensure that birdsong can survive at least, if not for her then for her dog Bear.

Both stories are an attempt, then, to resist the end, to ensure information survives so that humans (and perhaps non-humans through the recreation of birdsong) 'keep on' in some way, maintaining a through-line from pre-world to post-world. The use of such arguably gendered preapocalyptic activities as list-making and sculpture becoming one way that female characters try to navigate life in postapocalyptic landscapes.

References

Alber, Jan (2016), 'Absurd catalogues: The functions of lists in postmodernist fiction', *Style 1*, August, 50(3), pp. 342–358.

Atwood, Margaret (2011), 'Dire cartographies: The road to Ustopia', in *In Other Worlds: SF and the Human Imagination*, New York: Anchor Books, pp. 66–98.

Belknap, Robert (2000), 'The literary list: A survey of its uses and deployments', *Literary Imagination: The Review of the Association of Literary Scholars and Critics* 2(1), pp. 35–54.

Berger, James (1999), *After the End: Representations of Post-Apocalypse*, Minnesota: University of Minnesota Press.

Caracciolo, Marco (2018), 'Negative strategies and world disruption in postapocalyptic fiction', *Style* 52(3), pp. 222–241.

Curtis, Claire P. (2010), *Postapocalyptic Fiction and the Social Contract: 'We'll Not Go Home Again'*, Lanham, MD: Lexington Books/Fortress Academic.

Doyle, Briohny (2015), 'The postapocalyptic imagination', *Thesis Eleven* 131(1), pp. 99–113.

Instone, Alice (2024), *The pram in the hall.* Available at: https://www.aliceinstone.com/the-pram-in-the-hall (accessed 13 August 2024).

Le Guin, Ursula K. (2019), *Always Coming Home: Author's Expanded Edition,* New York: Library of America.

Machado, Carmen Maria (2019), *Her Body & Other Parties,* London: Serpent's Tail.

Payne, Mark (2020), *Flowers of Time: On Postapocalyptic Fiction,* Princeton, NJ: Princeton University Press.

Weida, Courtney Lee (2011), *Artistic Ambivalence in Clay: Portraits of Pottery, Ceramics, and Gender*, Newcastle upon Tyne: Cambridge Scholars Publishing.

Woman's Hour (2023), 'Lists: How and why we make them', BBC Radio 4, 28 August. Available at: https://www.bbc.co.uk/sounds/play/m001q0mt (accessed 13 August 2024).

Acknowledgements

A number of these stories have been published previously or been successful in prizes – thanks to editors and judges for selecting them. 'Maybe the birds' was shortlisted in Short Fiction's inaugural Wild Writing Prize and was published in *Short Fiction in Theory and Practice* alongside the critical article which forms the afterword; 'Leather' was published by Literati Magazine and selected for *Best British Short Stories 2021* (Salt Publishing); 'Piano' won the Negative Press London/Foyles Short Story Competition; 'One small thing' was published in *The Warwick Review* and reprinted in *Wall: Nine Stories from Edge Hill Writers*; 'Birthday' was published by *Fictive Dream*; 'Harbour lights' was commissioned for *The End: Fifteen Endings to Fifteen Paintings* (Unthank Books); 'The monolith' was published in *Unthology 3*.

With thanks to members of Edge Hill's Fiction Writers' Network for their support and feedback, as well as Neil Warren, Gaëlle Amiot-Cadey, Gill Blow, Lancaster University's staff writing group, my family and friends. Thanks also to The Society of Authors for funding.

This book is for my mum and my brother, for Chou, and is also in memory of my dad.

The Gold SF series

RECENT TITLES

Gold SF is a new imprint dedicated to discovering and publishing new intersectional feminist science fiction. Science fiction looks to the future and tries to imagine new ways of being in the world. Goldsmiths Press is a natural home for speculative fiction, and this new imprint promotes voices answering to our unprecedented times.

9781913380618

9781913380786

9781913380823

9781913380489

9781915983053

9781915983077

9781913380809

9781915983183

9781915983121

GOLD SF

Series editors *Una McCormack and Paul March-Russell*